AFTERMATH

Other books by Jerry S. Drake:

Sierra Skullduggery
The Gunfighter's Apprentice

AFTERMATH

•

Jerry S. Drake

AVALON BOOKS
NEW YORK

Published by Thomas Bouregy & Co., Inc.
160 Madison Avenue, New York, NY 10016

Library of Congress Cataloging-in-Publication Data

Drake, Jerry S.
  Aftermath / Jerry S. Drake.
     p. cm.
  ISBN 978-0-8034-9990-4
  I. Title.
  PS3604.R35A69 2009
  813'.6—dc22
          2009024252

PRINTED IN THE UNITED STATES OF AMERICA
ON ACID-FREE PAPER
BY HADDON CRAFTSMEN, BLOOMSBURG, PENNSYLVANIA

To family, friends, counselors, critics, and thoughtful advisors, my greatest gratitude for their help and support.

Chapter One

It was a place where they had played as small boys, an unexpected, odd plot of ground with a cluster of knobby hillocks eroded into curious, dramatic contours by a wandering stream. It was almost hidden by an enclosing swirl of cottonwood and poplar trees, a secret space for small, imaginative lads to make mounds and hummocks into battle summits against marauding Indians, ridges and knolls into fortifications against evil armies, or even shelters from the flaming breaths of scaly dragons.

On this morning in early June, it seemed a mystical place even now, Wallace Mitchell Ellsworth considered, as the ghost of remembrance touched him. He led his chestnut mare, Belle, down the bank to the brook, where she dipped her nose into the flowing water. It was right here he had "died" in melodramatic playacting from

1

make-believe bullets from Bobby Carlin's whittled-wood pistol. He furrowed his brow, recalling himself as a nine-year-old with a thick brush of corn-silk hair, staggering, holding his chest in imagined agony that became all too real as he tumbled down the embankment, his left arm thrust out at an awkward angle to keep him from rolling into the stream.

It all came back—the instant pain, the nausea as his childhood self stared at the jagged white bone gleaming through his bloodied forearm. He recalled the look of fright and dismay on his redheaded friend's face and the frantic scurry across the spring-plowed field to his home.

Now, beneath his shirtsleeve, he fingered the ridge of the scar and remembered the gasp and tears of his mother, the frightened wails of his younger sister, and the stern calm of his father. Jacob Ellsworth had given neither reprimand nor admonishment; he had cushioned his son in the bed of the buckboard and driven him three miles into the small western Missouri village of Mayfield. With care and reassurances, his father carried him up the stairs to the doctor's office over the settlement's only pharmacy.

"Bad break for young Wally," Doc Davis had muttered as he examined the arm. "Hope I can fix it."

"Call me Mitch," he remembered saying. "I'm no Wally."

"What's wrong with Wally?" the doctor asked.

"One kid called me Walrus at school," he said. "But he only did it that one time."

The remark brought a chuckle to the doctor and even to his father.

Mitch grimaced as he remembered the pain—the doctor and his father straining to pull the bone ends apart and then join them together as best they could—before Doc Davis splinted and immobilized the arm.

"Much good you'll be in helping with the crops," his father had said gruffly, giving a wink to the doctor, although he wasn't speaking entirely in jest. "Getting too old to be playing little-kid games."

How long since he had seen Bobby? Ten years?

When Belle lifted her head from the stream, Mitch led the mare to a tree where she could graze on thick green grass. He looked around and realized the grove was not exactly the same as before. Some of the poplars—trees that matured swiftly and as quickly died—were gone, smaller sprouts taking their places.

Mitch removed his wide-brimmed hat and ran a hand over his thinning hair. Not only were the trees of yesteryear gone, but much of his youth was as well. He was only thirty-one, but he had a lifetime's worth of remorse. He gave his horse a comforting pat and walked her to a place in the shade, feeling the warmth of the summer sun filtering through the leaves.

"Mitch, you're getting old—sleeping in the shade."

Mitch looked up at Robert Carlin, and, for just a moment, time fell away. Still slim and straight, his face and jawline seemingly unchanged, he looked much as he had a decade before.

"Come on, soldier, up and about now," Bob said, bending down.

The illusion shattered. Bob's face was still handsome, but the fine lines around his eyes and deeper ones around his mouth gave a hint of something unsettling.

"Good to see you, Bob," Mitch said, rising. He held out a hand.

"I didn't know if you'd actually come," Carlin said, clasping Mitch's hand and drawing him into an embrace. Then he thrust him back to study his face. "Lordy, I'm glad to see you."

"It's been a spell," Mitch said, with a smile.

"Long trip?"

"Couple of days' ride."

"You an old married man now?"

"No, ladies are a little leery of former jailbirds. How about you?"

"No wife, no young 'uns, nothing to tie me down."

"When did you get out?"

"Almost a year now," Carlin said, and he turned to the six men standing with their horses a short distance behind him. "Look who I've got with me."

Mitch followed Carlin's gaze to the group. Five were young men, unkempt, surly looking. The sixth, a burly middle-ager with a gap-toothed grin, surged forward a few steps.

"Hi, Mitch, it's me . . . Hubie!"

"Lord bless us, Hubert McGinnis!" Mitch responded. "How've you been?"

"Just fine, just fine," the man said happily, childlike in his speech and manner. He started forward again. "It's gonna be just like old times, Mitch. You and me and Bobby and—"

Carlin cut a sharp look at the hefty, ebullient man.

Instantly Hubie stopped, his head down. "Sorry, Captain."

" 'Captain?' " Mitch questioned, followed by a grunt of incredulity.

Carlin smiled. "Well, the men call me that . . . and I like the sound of it."

"Just who *are* these men . . . other than Hubie?"

"Young fellows working for me."

"Work? What kinda work?"

"Work that got interrupted some years back."

Mitch studied his friend for a long, silent period and then sighed. "Well, *Captain,* the war's been over a long time." He sighed. "Down deep I sort of worried it might be something like this. I shouldn't have come."

"But you did."

"My mistake. I thought you might be needing some help, something like getting a new start."

Carlin gave an emphatic nod. "I *do* need help—another man I can really count on. These young ones are long on wanting but short on know-how."

"Those days are history, thank the good Lord," Mitch said wearily. "I spent eight years in the Jeff City pen for the banks and trains we did after the war . . . but I don't do that anymore."

"I spent nearly ten in an Arkansas hellhole—two more than you. I mean to make up for that."

"What you'll do is get yourself right back into prison, Bob," Mitch said.

Carlin didn't respond for several seconds. "You making a good life for yourself?" he said finally.

"Some. Working for wages, but I got my eye on a nice little farm over near Lebanon that I might make into something."

"Hell's bells, forget farming. Come do this job with me, and then we'll head south, sit under some palm trees, and do some easy living."

Mitch gave a sigh of dismay. "What fool thing are you talking about? You robbing a bank?"

Carlin gave a wide, confident grin. "Our very own stomping grounds, right over next door there in Harrisonville. They got a whole lot of money in that town, and they keep it all at the bank. There's not much law, and they've got only a one-armed duffer standing guard. It'll be damned easy."

Mitch shook his head.

"Ah, come on, Mitch, I need you," Carlin implored. "Nobody's gonna know it's you or me after all this time. We come trickling in by ones and twos, cover our faces, walk in, and just help ourselves."

"No," Mitch said. "I want no part of it."

"It's only going to be this one time. From what I hear,

there's plenty enough that we won't ever have to do it again. It'll be a chance for you and me to buy a new start on our lives."

"What about them?" Mitch asked, nodding to the group behind his friend.

"They'll get their shares," Carlin assured him. "Plenty for all . . . easy pickings."

"And what if something goes wrong, and innocent people get hurt or maybe killed?" He paused. "Want something like that on your conscience?"

Carlin fell silent for a few moments, then spoke. "You suddenly got the calling? Got religion? 'Do unto others . . .' How's that saying go?"

Abruptly one of the men standing apart snickered. "Maybe he's afraid *he's* the one that's gonna get hurt." The speaker, a narrow-faced young man with bad, pallid skin and a churlish manner, spoke again. "We don't need him, Captain. Don't need no Holy Roller riding with us."

"Hold your tongue, Nate," Carlin said sharply. "You're talking to a friend of mine, a gallant comrade in arms." He paused. "Comrades forever . . . Didn't we say that years ago right here in this very spot?"

"Wasting your breath, *Captain* Bob," Mitch said. "You've been warned."

"Warned?" Carlin's expression grew stern.

Mitch nodded. "Yes, a warning for your sake. Don't do it, Bob. Back then, even after Lee gave it up, we thought we had a reason, a cause to do what we did." He shook his head. "They went light on us because of what had been done to us during the war, taking away our folks' property and all. It won't be like that anymore. This time it'll be a hanging."

"I'm doing it. With or without you."

"When?"

"Today, as a matter of fact," Carlin said. "We were on our way when we stopped by to see if you'd show."

"I should've known better," Mitch said angrily. "You're on a fool's trip to the graveyard."

"You ain't going to let him walk away, are you, Captain?" The narrow-faced young man took several steps forward, moving past Hubie, his right hand hovering near the Colt revolver in his hip holster. "He'll run straight for the law."

Mitch turned slightly, his eyes locking on those of the agitator. The intensity blazed for a moment between them. Then the young man's gaze dropped to the ground, and he shuffled back.

"That's what I need," Carlin said with a chuckle. "A steady hand to hold the reins on these young bucks."

"They look like a bad lot, Bob," Mitch said. "They'll shoot somebody when it isn't necessary, and they'll hightail it and run at the first sign of trouble."

"Well, they're better'n they look and the best I can do for the time being," Carlin said. "Once again, Mitch, come along—for old time's sake."

Mitch shook his head. "No, Bob."

Carlin did not react immediately. His dour expression remained for a few moments and then relaxed into an easy smile. "All right, Mitch. I wish I could say I didn't care, but you know I do."

Mitch was not disarmed by the smile. Too many times in his early life, that smile had persuaded.

"You'll keep your mouth shut about what we're doing?" Carlin questioned, a look of concern on his face.

Mitch didn't respond, not knowing the answer.

"You gonna let him ride out?" Nate called, belligerence returning.

"You want to stop him?" Carlin countered.

The youth glowered and turned away.

"Better watch that one, Bob," Mitch said. "He'll likely back-shoot you one day."

"Never had to worry about that in the old days," his friend responded.

Mitch offered his right hand. "Sorry, Bob. It's just that I'm . . . different now."

Carlin took his hand in a strong clasp and put an affectionate left hand on Mitch's shoulder. "Wish us good luck, partner."

"I wish you better sense, Bob," Mitch responded. "For old time's sake, I'm asking you, don't go on with it." He watched Carlin's face for a few seconds and saw no change in the pleasant, smiling face.

He pulled away, turned to shake Hubie's hand, and then went to his horse. He reached for the reins and hesitated. Instinct made him draw his gun and whirl, and by doing so, he dodged instant death. The impact of the bullet slammed him against a tree and jarred the Colt revolver from his hand as his one shot went wild, missing the narrow-faced outlaw entirely. As he slid to the ground, he saw that young man held no weapon. He was puzzling on that when the pain enveloped him. It was somewhere in his torso and becoming a monstrous, dreadful burn welling from inside. He wanted to scream, but the hurt was so severe, he couldn't pass breath over his vocal cords. He tumbled and rolled facedown in the grass.

My God! Did I do this to people? Let me die, dear God. Let me die!

"Bobby! What did you do?" It was Hubie's voice, high and reproving. "You killed him, Bobby! You killed him!"

"Stop bellerin' about it," Carlin responded.

Lying still in spite of his agony, Mitch was acutely aware of his horse contentedly grazing a few feet away, the excited voices, the sound of the stream, the wind stirring the leaves, a crow cawing high above.

"Where you going, Bobby? Don't you shoot him again!"

There was a long silence.

"Had to shoot him, Hubie. He could've told about us."

"He wouldn't have! You killed him—your friend, my friend!"

"It's done. Make sure." Carlin's voice grew strong with command. "You tell me if he's dead, and don't you lie to me."

Mitch tried to keep his breathing shallow, hoping the high grass would hide the subtle rise and fall of his chest. He fixed his eyes on a single blade of grass and hoped his vacant stare would appear a death glaze. He forced himself not to glance up as Hubie knelt beside him. The big man's blunt fingers touched his face gently, tenderly.

Mitch realized that Hubie knew. Simple man or not, he had seen too many deaths to be fooled.

"Well?" Carlin called.

Hubie hesitated for a moment. "He's gone, Bobby. He's shot plumb dead—and you done it!"

"Put a shot through his head, Hubie!"

It was the narrow-faced youth.

"Do it, Hubie," Carlin instructed. "Can't hurt him if he's dead."

"I won't!"

"Do it, or I will," Carlin persisted.

A surge of pain coursed through Mitch's belly, and he willed himself to remain still.

Do it, Hubie, before the pain comes again.

He heard Hubie's gun cock and felt the cold muzzle held to his right temple. The shot was a cannon blast, and his entire body spasmed, bucking in shock before he fell still again. Miraculously, his senses remained, his right ear blown deaf, but his eyes still focused on the grass blades an inch away.

Still alive!

With his good ear, he could hear Hubie weeping— long, shuddering intakes of breath that evidenced genuine grief. *Better actor than Booth. Who would have thought?*

Mitch's head began to hurt, but it was the sharp, superficial burn of a singed scalp and gunpowder peppering.

"All right, Hubie, let's ride," Carlin instructed.

"Can I bury him, Captain?"

"Leave him. Someone will find him."

"Let me stay, please!"

Mitch's senses began to blur, and the blades of grass fuzzed into darkness. He tried to remain awake, but the voices were distant and garbled.

Then the darkness overwhelmed him.

Chapter Two

Mitch awoke a bit and experienced pain coming in waves, agonizing, then subsiding. He could locate the wound now, a pulsing in his right side just below the rib cage. A little more to the center, the shot would have been to his heart; lower, he would have been gut-shot. He wasn't sure he hadn't been.

Bad, but maybe not too bad—be dead by now if it was.

He lay still, listening. There were the sounds of the stream, the rustling wind, even a high-wheeling crow. The men were gone.

Weakly he untied the tan bandanna from around his neck, unbuttoned his shirt, and grimaced at the sight of the blood-seeping wound. He wadded the bandanna against the dark red puncture and held his left hand hard against it.

He tried to pull himself up, and the first effort brought

him close to fainting again. He rested and then tried again, gingerly inching up on his arms, keeping the strain off his torso. After a struggle, he managed to sit upright against the trunk of a tree.

His horse remained at the stream, not drinking, just standing. His revolver lay five feet away. He looked at it and wanted it in his hand. For years now he had carried it out of habit with no thought of using it. Now he wanted to use it, badly, perhaps on himself.

It took five minutes to crawl to the revolver, another five to get to his horse. He rested on the ground, reins in hand, the gun in his holster. He knew it would take whatever strength he had left to pull himself up into the saddle. It might be impossible.

"I gotta try," he said aloud.

Luckily, his mare didn't shy away. Belle stood still as he hooked his right arm into the left-side stirrup and levered himself to a kneeling position. He felt his surroundings swimming again, and he rested until the sensation lessened slightly. As a small amount of strength returned, he reached higher to the D ring on the saddle and pulled himself up to a woozy, upright stance.

So much for the easy part.

With a gasp of pain, he released his grip on the D ring and stretched his right hand to grasp the saddle horn. He took his bloody left hand from his wound and, bending in agony, reached to lift his left leg at the knee and guided the booted foot into the stirrup.

Now, the hard part.

Raising his other hand to the saddle horn, he coiled his body and pulled hard, surging upward.

For the first time, Mitch cried aloud, a guttural howl as pain coursed through him. Vaguely he was aware that his intense effort was only partially successful. His right leg was precariously draped high across the left slope of the horse's rump. He had to pull it over the middle or lose his tenuous position. If the horse moved or if his leg slid an inch or two back, he would be on the ground again—a hard fall and probably a fatal one.

Slowly, determinedly, he stretched his right leg across the rump and down, exhilaration flooding him as he hooked his heel into the stirrup on the other side and settled into the saddle.

Sat a horse better, but this'll do.

Pressing his left hand to his wound again, he waited a few minutes before reaching for and retrieving the reins. In doing so, he fainted again.

A few seconds later he regained consciousness and guided the horse out of the woodland glen. In the heat of the late-morning sun, he was absolutely spent, exhausted, relying more on instinct than rational thought. He dimly realized that now, out of the grove, he desperately needed immediate medical aid, but how to get it was a vague notion without a sense of direction. The rhythmic movements of the slow-walking horse rocked and lulled him in and out of consciousness. Black waves ebbed and flowed and gave way at last to the void that eclipsed his mind and body. Mitch Ellsworth lay sprawled across the saddle as Belle ambled gently through the sun-baked meadow of his yesteryears.

Mitch came to again as the horse moved out of the hot sun into the shade of trees surrounding a house that swam in vague familiarity in his clouded vision. He lay across the saddle, his face against the warm horsehair of Belle's neck, and realized a sense of homecoming.

My arm, Ma! I'm hurt bad, but Bobby got me home! Tell Pa! Tell Pa!

He raised his head with effort and looked around. The familiar setting had somehow changed. The paint on his childhood house was flaking, and the outbuildings were gray and splintered with age. Somehow, even in the black void of unconsciousness, he had guided Belle to his child-hood home. At the back porch, someone moved behind the shining screen door.

"Help me!" he called in little more than a hoarse whisper. "Help me, please."

"Who are you? What do you want here?" It was a woman's voice, strong with irritation and anxiety.

"Help me!" he pleaded, putting what strength he had left into his voice. "I don't know where else to go."

The woman came out of the door and down the two steps, a rifle in her hands, the stock near her shoulder. In the doorway behind her a youngster not yet in his teens stood watching.

"What's wrong with you?" she demanded, moving closer, the rifle rising higher.

"Been shot, ma'am," he managed to say. "I need help."

The woman put the rifle to her shoulder and took careful aim. "Throw down your handgun."

Mitch reacted slowly and reached for the revolver at his side. As he did so, a wave of pain and dizziness overcame him. Hazily he put his hand to the saddle horn to steady himself in the saddle, but black shadows swooped down and engulfed him.

His senses returned slowly and filled him with confusion. He was lying on something soft, yet he felt the hard surface beneath. He realized he was, somehow, in motion; he experienced a swaying, a creaking of turning wheels, and the hard, hurtful jolt of those wheels dropping into road cavities.

He was in a wagon, lying on a blanket, another over him. Through blurry eyes he could see a woman and a boy on the wagon seat above him. He tried to raise his head. "Where am I?"

"Lie still," the woman said sharply. "You're hurt bad, and I'm taking you to town to the doctor."

"How bad?" he murmured.

The woman turned her head to look down at him, a pretty face somewhat tinged by fading youth and now frowning with concern and suspicion. "You've lost a lot of blood. You nearly fell off your horse, and I thought you were dead." She turned away to snap the reins and hurry the horse pulling the wagon. "I put a patch on you, but that was the best I could do."

Mitch tried to offer his thanks, but he sank once more into the void.

When he stirred again, he was inside a room that reeked of chemicals. He was lying on a flat leather surface, staring up at a hanging lantern burning brightly. Three walls of the room were crowded with breakfronts topped with glass enclosures that displayed a variety of bottles, tins, and flasks. The fourth side of the room included a double door, one closed, the other open, allowing a partial view of a combined office and waiting room. Against the daylight of a distant window he could see the silhouettes of the woman who had helped him and a vaguely familiar, stoop-shouldered, frail old man. They spoke in low voices.

Doc Davis, still alive?

He strained to hear.

". . . lost a lot of blood . . . not likely to . . ."

". . . didn't know what to do . . . seemed like the only Christian thing . . ."

". . . go on home . . ."

Time was a haze, a vaguely recalled hodgepodge of his clothes being removed, of the older man bending over him with hands touching, of something metal probing his wound, of scalding liquid heightening the blaze of his injury. Intermittent periods of awareness blended with the abyss of nonexistence.

The heat and glare of intense sunlight and the clamor of many voices brought Mitch around, his eyelids fluttering against the invasion. He seemed to be in a slanted, upright position, gravity pulling at him, something pressing up under each armpit to prevent his collapse. He was somehow pinned against a hard wooden surface with pine planks surrounding him.

I'm in . . . a box?

He tried to raise his right hand to shade his eyes, but the effort was beyond his strength, his fingers touching the bandages on his torso before falling again to his side. Still, he used those fingers to explore what was at his side, and his mind eventually identified the wooden object. *A crutch! One on each side, under my armpits, to prop me up in a . . . a what? A coffin?*

Squinting against the dazzling afternoon sunlight, he could see men, women, and little boys and girls all standing in an arc around him in the center of a street. The images swayed and danced in a great gray mist, and he glimpsed a man behind a bulky wooden camera on a tripod, his head and shoulders hidden beneath a dark cloth, his hands reaching to adjust the length of the bellows. Then the brilliant light blurred into darkness, and his consciousness plunged back into the abyss.

Chapter Three

The street was empty and nearly as dark as his long spells of coma. The chill of the late night had brought him awake once again, and he was surprised that he was still alive. His awareness was stronger than before, perhaps stimulated by the damp cold on his bare chest and shoulders. A single lantern hanging from a distant pole gave dim illumination to a dirt road that ran through the center of a small settlement, and only a few lamps shone in a handful of buildings.

Perhaps, instead, it was the creaking wheels of an approaching wagon that had roused him, or the low voices of the people with it. He could see the ebony silhouettes of the farmwife and her boy on the wagon seat, while three dark figures walked behind the cart. The wagon stopped in front of him, and the woman leaned down to speak softly, anxiously. "Is he still alive, Doc?"

Mitch felt the urge to speak but remained silent, wary.

A stooped figure shuffled close and leaned toward him. "Seems so, and it's a wonder why," Dr. Davis ventured in his aged wheeze. "Just barely."

"Should we be doing this, Doc?" A lean silhouette stepped forward. "We thought he was dead."

"He's close to it, Howard," the physician said. "You and Tim put him in the wagon. Mrs. Jennings is Christian enough to offer him a bed to die in and some care and comfort while he does. He won't last long, and he'll get nothing but dreadful treatment if we leave him here in town."

The other man started to protest. "I don't know, Doc. He's one of that gang—"

"I know who he is and what he is," the doctor cut in. "I've known him since he was a boy. He was once a good lad, and, no matter what he's done, he deserves better than this."

"Well, maybe the marshal should—"

"That drunken sot!" The woman spoke unexpectedly. "Leaving this man in the middle of the street to die while *he's* carousing and passed out in a saloon!" She paused, her anger subsiding. "I think this man came to his home— my home now—to die."

"We could take him back up to your office, Doc," the man called Tim said.

"Not with that redleg scum with a badge in charge," the doctor retorted in scorn. "I couldn't keep him from dragging the patient out of my office for the damned picture before. How can I prevent it again?"

"Ain't there any good people in town you can count on, Doc?" the man named Howard asked.

"I'm hoping you are two of 'em," the doctor responded. "Just so you don't borrow trouble, if you're asked about him, tell them I said he was dead and released his body to Mrs. Jennings to bury in his family plot."

There were several moments of silence.

"I don't know, Doc," Howard persisted. "I don't want to take no chances with Marshal Langley. He's a damned mean man."

"Howard," the doctor said with a sigh, "I took chances every day for over a week tending to your missus when she had the cholera."

The silhouette bowed his head.

"Saved your boy's leg when it got infected, Tim," Dr. Davis said to the other shadow.

"We owe you, Doc," Tim admitted, and his companion nodded.

"I hate to have to collect, but I'm asking now," the old man said.

"We ain't the only ones taking chances," Tim said, and he turned his head to the woman on the wagon. "You'd be taking a mighty risk, ma'am, taking him into your home. He ain't no good, from what I hear."

"Load him into the back, and be careful with him," she instructed.

"Leave him in the coffin?" Tim asked.

"Land's sakes, no!"

"You want it for the burying?" the same man asked.

The woman hesitated. "I suppose you might as well. I may need it."

"Need us to come dig the hole?" Howard asked reluctantly.

"I'll send word if and when the time comes."

"What if he gets better?" Tim wanted to know.

"I guess I'll have to send word to that no-account marshal. I need to get home, so you'd best get on with it."

Tim unfastened the tailgate of the wagon and then joined Howard as they walked to lift Mitch out of the coffin. With their shoulders under each of his arms, they carried him to the end of the wagon. As they struggled to maneuver him into the wagon bed, Mitch caught a glimpse of a still figure in a second tilted coffin next to the one he had occupied.

He groaned.

"Sorry, fellow," one of the silhouettes said. "Rest easy, now."

A few seconds later Mitch felt the coffin sliding in alongside him, its wooden bottom scraping the wagon bed.

"Thank you both," Dr. Davis said. "I've got your money, and—"

"Ain't no need, Doc," Howard said quickly, and he turned to the woman on the wagon seat. "You've got a good heart, Mrs. Jennings, but you be careful of this man. You got a gun at your place and know how to use it?"

"My husband taught me well," she assured him as she snapped the reins to start the horse forward. "Thank you once again."

"You gonna die, mister?"

Mitch gritted his teeth against the jolting pain that came with every turn of the wagon wheels on the bumpy road. He opened his eyes to the vault of a starry night sky and then glanced to meet the gaze of the boy looking down at him. "Try not to," he said, his voice hoarse and whispery.

"Leave him alone, Andy!" his mother said sharply. She turned to look back. "You're awake?"

"Have been," Mitch croaked. "Some of the time."

"The boy asked a good question. Think you're going to die?"

"I don't know."

"The fact that you're talking is a good sign," she said, glancing back at the road. "You heard the men back there?"

Mitch didn't answer.

"If you heard, you know they said I'm taking a fool's chance with you," she said, her voice hard. "Truth is, I *did* expect you to pass on."

"Not far from it," he muttered.

"We're almost home," she said. "*My* home."

Mitch started to answer, but the stars began to blur, and he couldn't quite remember what he was going to say.

Chapter Four

Mitch came awake to the cheer of sunlight beaming through a window and inching across a coverlet toward his face. His shoulders were bare, and he realized he was naked to the waist beneath a light quilt, something feeling like pajama trousers on his lower body. He recognized his surroundings, although the furniture was different; it was his mother's sewing room at the back of the house on the ground floor. It had been converted to a sitting room with bookcases and a small rolltop desk. There were landscape paintings on the walls and a scattering of sepia photographic prints. One caught his eye, a formal wedding pose of a very young woman and a handsome yet far older man in a Union officer's tunic.

A sofa covered by sheets and the coverlet served him as a bed. Through an open door he could see the kitchen and the living room. The layout of the home seemed familiar yet alien, with different furnishings and arrangements. Even so, childhood memories came flooding back. In the kitchen, the tall floor-to-ceiling cupboards looked years older, and the oiled plank flooring bore the wear of his family's and the later occupants' boots and shoes.

The Jennings woman stepped into the doorway, a dust mop in her hands and a kerchief tied about her hair. "You're clearheaded?"

Mitch shifted his position and was startled to discover his right hand manacled to the underside frame of the divan. He peered down and examined the foot-long chain that gave him a limited range of movement but secured him effectively.

"Sorry about that," the woman half apologized. "But it seemed the prudent thing to do."

Mitch lay back and nodded. "I can't blame you. How did you get me inside?"

"Andy and I managed," she told him. "You even walked a little."

With his left hand he touched the stubble of beard on his face. "How long have I been out?"

"This is the third morning," she told him. "You've been in and out at times, but you don't remember." She paused. "I'm Mrs. Jennings."

"Yes, ma'am," he responded. "I'm—"

"Mitchell Ellsworth," she interrupted. "Notorious in this community. You and your friend Carlin rode with Quantrill's cutthroats and then were outlaws after the war."

He shrugged.

"Are you hungry? Would you like something to eat?"

"Yes, ma'am, I'd appreciate it, if it's not too much trouble."

"You're well-spoken," she said, "for a ruffian."

"I'm also housebroken."

She smiled, a pleasant expression that brought a youthful beauty to her face. "I'll fix you something, but it ought to be soft. Some eggs, some milk—nothing to upset your stomach."

"Suppose I could have some coffee?"

"Maybe you could try a little. I'll be back in a few minutes."

He watched her as she walked to the kitchen stove, where she reached for a lifter, opened the lid, and stirred the glowing embers to a brighter burn. She disappeared from sight for a few seconds and then returned to the stove. "Can you handle two eggs?"

"Fried if you wouldn't mind, ma'am," Mitch responded.

Even at a distance he could see again the smile of good humor as she shook her head. "How about poached? Fried might be hard to digest."

"Whatever you say, ma'am."

Several minutes later she came into the room carrying a tray with a plate of soft-cooked eggs, a glass of milk, and a mug of coffee. She placed the tray on a low table and moved it close to the divan. "Can you sit up?"

"Maybe," he said. He made the effort, grimacing at the pain in his side.

She pulled a chair up close and sat down near him. "Can you feed yourself?"

He reached for the spoon on the tray with his right hand, chagrined as the chain stopped the motion. He reached with his left.

"How do you feel?" she asked.

"Like I've been shot," he said as he clumsily cut an egg with the edge of the spoon in his left hand and, trembling, scooped a morsel from the plate and guided it to his mouth. He glanced at the handcuffs again. "Just happened to have this lying around?"

"The men who put you in the wagon thought it was wise," she replied. "They put it in the coffin."

"The coffin," Mitch repeated. "I'm not feeling all that good, but I don't think it was quite time to measure me for that." He took another bite of the egg, laid down the spoon, and reached for the coffee mug. "In the town, when they had me propped up in one, what in the world were they doing?"

"Taking a picture for history, they said," she answered. "Pictures of you and a dead man who was one of those who robbed the bank over in Harrisonville. There was shooting after they came out of the bank, and an innocent man, a bank customer, was killed. One of the robbers was shot, too, but he made it to Mayfield before he fell dead off his horse."

"Who was he?"

"Last name was McGinnis, they say," she supplied.

"Hubie," Mitch said with regret. "Hubert McGinnis." He paused and then asked, "What about the rest of them?"

"Most got away, I hear." She regarded him closely. "It was your old bunch of outlaws, wasn't it? The Carlin gang?"

"Different bunch. Most, I didn't know."

"But you did ride with Carlin, didn't you?"

"Not for years." He looked at her face to judge her reaction. "And I didn't this time."

"I know," she said with a nod.

Her answer surprised him. "How?"

"From what I've been told, about the time you came to my place, they were just showing up at the Harrisonville bank," she told him. "You'd have had to have wings to be in both places at the same time."

"I'm surely no angel," he said with a wry grin.

She didn't return the smile. "Did you see them that day?"

Mitch sat quietly for several seconds. "Yes, ma'am, early on," he admitted. "Bob Carlin, a friend I grew up with, he sent me a note saying he needed my help." He paused for another few moments. "I thought, perhaps, he was talking about getting a start on a new life."

"And?"

Mitch shook his head. "He wanted me to help him rob another bank."

This time the woman was silent for a while.

"I told him no." Mitch said. "And they really didn't like my answer."

"Were they the ones who shot you?"

He nodded.

Her face grew grave. She sighed. "I brought you to town about the same time the other outlaw showed up. Everyone assumed you were one too."

Mitch smiled and took a drink of milk. "You didn't tell 'em different?"

"I wasn't sure 'til later," she told him. "And once I figured out the time situation, I couldn't get anyone to listen."

"The town marshal?"

She exhaled her exasperation. "A stupid man, and a nasty one too. He was with a Union guerrilla outfit in the war, those who wore those dreadful red leggings. He knew your reputation of riding with Quantrill and then the outlaws, and he wanted to make an example of you and the other fellow." She looked closely at him. "Hearing about that man's death bothered you, didn't it?"

"I'm alive because of him. He was supposed to finish me off, but he faked it, and Bob Carlin believed him."

"I'm sorry, then. Maybe he wasn't all bad."

"He wasn't too bright, but he shouldn't have ever teamed up with Bob." He paused. "Or me."

"Can you eat any more?"

Mitch shook his head. "Sitting up nearly wore me out."

She rose from her chair and picked up the tray. "Lie

back and rest. Doc Davis did a good job of patching you up. He said the bullet went clean through and didn't hit anything vital, but you did lose a lot of blood. You'll have to be careful."

"I expect that that nasty lawman you talked about ought to be stopping by any time now," he said as he lay back on the divan.

"Been here and gone."

He looked at her in wonderment.

She chuckled. "Andy and I turned some dirt and made a wooden cross to put on it out there in your old family plot."

"He didn't come into the house or check the grave?"

She shook her head. "He's far too lazy to bother."

"Won't that mean trouble for you if he finds out different?"

She shrugged. "If he ever finds out, I'll deal with it." She nodded out the window. "As soon as you can ride, you ought to go."

Mitch lifted the coverlet and looked at the wide bandage taped to his side. He saw only a small trace of seeped blood, and the surrounding flesh appeared of a normal color, no visible red streaks of infection spreading from the wound. "Why would you take such a chance by helping me?" he asked as he lowered the quilt.

"Call it my guilt, I suppose."

"Guilt?" Mitch took a deep breath that hurt his side. "I don't understand."

"I live in a house that was taken by my husband's

folks from yours," she said as she paused in the doorway. "I was curious about your family and about you. What happened to your family?"

"Alive and resettled over in Lebanon in the middle of the state. My father works at a lumberyard, and my mother teaches grade school. My sister's married and living nearby."

"I hope they've done well. They deserve a better time." She paused. "From what I learned, I can't say that I approve of what you did during and after the war, but I did sort of understand it." She swept her gaze around the room, then shrugged her shoulders as if to rid herself of her feelings. "We took this house that shouldn't have belonged to us."

For a long period of contemplation, Mitch was silent.

"I don't know if you're a good man or a bad one, but I'm the only one left here to do something right," she said. "You should leave as soon as you're able and get out of this part of the country once and for all."

He struggled to sit up again. "If you'll fetch me my clothes—"

"We'll risk another night's rest," she cut in; then she turned and walked into the kitchen.

Mitch rested his head on the pillow and stared at the ceiling until weariness dissolved into a deep and gentle slumber.

Chapter Five

In their early adolescence, Mitch and Bobby had become increasingly aware of the prewar turmoil in their Missouri and Kansas border region. The slave state and free state status of each boiled the blood of zealots on the other side of North and South issues. Both the Ellsworth and the Carlin families lived on adjacent farms in an area bordering the Kansas line often called Little Dixie. Although slavery, as in the southernmost eastern states, was a major concern in Missouri, the subject of states' rights was also paramount. Many people in the area, while neither slave owners nor advocates of human bondage, sympathized with other Southern issues. Farm families often had friends and relations who rode with the southern raiders or aided, fed, supplied, and sheltered them.

Tempers escalated in both states as Bushwhackers from Missouri made murderous forays into Kansas, and Jayhawkers retaliated with lethal raids of their own. With the onset of the Civil War, violence came to a fury on the border. By only a very narrow decision, the state leaders of Missouri declined to join the Confederacy and, to the dismay of many, remained in the Union. However, a significant portion of its citizens along the border escalated their involvement with those who raided Kansas localities. The Ellsworth family, southern in their thinking although not in agreement with the slavery issue, tried to stay detached.

"It'll blow over," Jacob Ellsworth had said to calm his wife, Jennifer, his small daughter, Emma, and his son of barely fourteen years, Mitch. "The main fighting's going to keep on back east, away from here. We're staying out of it."

Then, on August 21, 1863, William Clarke Quantrill, a nefarious felon and a self-proclaimed Confederate officer, led a horde of rebel irregulars into Lawrence, Kansas. They burned, plundered, and destroyed the town. As many as 150 men, many of them helpless and unarmed, were dragged from their homes and killed in front of their families. To border Kansans, it was a day of atrocities, while to many border Missourians, it was a daring reprisal for Jayhawker killings in the sporadic western conflict.

Four days later Brigadier General Thomas Ewing Jr. of the Union Army, commander of this border region, issued Order Number 11. Under this ruthless directive, farm families in four border counties, rightly or wrongly suspected as supporters or sympathizers of the Confederacy, were to be forcibly evicted from their homes. In reprisal for the Lawrence atrocity, scores of farmers and their families had their houses and buildings burned, their livestock and personal properties confiscated and ofttimes awarded to scavenging opportunists.

Eleven days after Quantrill's raid, a squad of troopers from the 13th Kansas Cavalry rode through the gate into the yard of the Ellsworth farm, plumes of smoke rising in the surrounding countryside. Flames were leaping from the neighboring Carlin property, the naked chimney occasionally visible through the swirling black smoke.

Leaving his wife, son, and daughter on the porch behind him, Jacob Ellsworth moved down the steps and strode toward the young Union officer on horseback in the lead of the riders. He came within five feet of the officer and looked up, his shoulders held straight and a look of righteous indignation on his face. "May I have your name, sir?"

"Lieutenant Joe Bill Hawkins," the officer replied, a smirk on his narrow, sunburned face. He was nothing more than a callow youth, sweating in his dirty blue uniform.

"This is a monstrous thing you are about, Lieutenant."

"Are you packed and ready to leave?" the youthful officer asked.

"No, sir," Jacob answered. "We want to explain—"

"Then get about it!" the officer cut in. "We'll give you an hour."

"We aren't leaving," Jacob responded resolutely. "We are innocent people. We've had no part in what has happened. This is our property, and we ask you to leave."

The officer drew his side arm. "One hour, or I'll kill you where you stand."

"That will be on your conscience!"

The officer aimed his revolver.

"No, Jacob!" came the cry from his wife, who rushed from the porch into the yard, Mitch and his sister right behind her. "Tell him we'll go!"

"He's too much of a coward to kill me, Jennifer," Jacob said. "Go back to the house."

The officer laughed, showing a gap in his unbrushed, irregular teeth. His gaze traveled to the youngsters standing behind the woman. "I'll shoot the boy as well." He paused and returned his eyes to Jacob. "And I'll put you and your womenfolk to walking the road with nothing but whatcha can carry."

Jacob's pose of defiance faltered as he glanced back at his family.

"We've got to go, Jacob," his wife pleaded. "Do what he says . . . please!"

Jacob gave a huge sigh and looked once again with anger at the young officer. "All right, burn us out, you damned Yankee. We'll go. Leave my family alone, and we'll go."

The oafish officer raised his eyes to appraise the sturdy

farmhouse and then swept his gaze to the barn. "We need a place to quarter." He nodded. "This'll do fine."

With just a few minutes before the harsh deadline, the Ellsworth family was woefully unprepared for departure. A few of Jennifer's keepsakes along with Jacob's tools and other miscellaneous household items had been loaded onto the buckboard to be pulled by their oldest and nearly decrepit mare, the only one allowed them from their stable of fine horses.

On the dirt road that ran past their property and their neighbors', three wagons were slowly approaching. To the jeers and taunts of the surrounding Union soldiers, Jacob urged the animal out of the gate to fall in line behind the Carlin family's wagon as it passed by. With tears not only in the eyes of the mother and daughter but also glistening in those of Jacob and Mitch, the terrible departure began. The adolescent boy sat in the bed of the buckboard with his little sister, and they held hands as they looked back at the house, the homestead of their birth and comfortable childhood.

For a couple of miles the Ellsworth and Carlin families traveled in a short convoy. At a major east-west road, their wagons were joined by several others turning east, none toward Kansas. It was a sad parade of heartbreak and despair as families from the four indicted counties moved toward the center of Missouri. Only a handful of days had transformed these people from landowning respectability and self-sufficiency to ignominy and abject poverty. Once out of the immediate vicinity of Union au-

thoritarianism, the individual wagons, buggies, and buck-
boards split off toward various destinations as different
families sought sanctuary wherever it might or might not
exist.

For Mitch's family, their slim chance of survival lay in
the small Missouri town of Lebanon in the lower middle
section of the state. Their desperate hope was that his
mother's younger sister, Mildred Coleman, who lived
there with her husband, Ben, and their three small children, could possibly take them in.

After five days of miserable travel with little money,
food, or shelter from the hot days and a drenching
mid-September rainfall, they arrived at the four-room
house, where they were given a single room for shelter.

"I wish we could do more," Ben Coleman said with
regret.

"We're barely making ends meet," his wife, Mildred,
said tearfully.

"We appreciate what you are doing," Jacob said. "A
night or two, maybe, that's all we'll be."

The Carlin family, camped outside the small village
for three days, had decided to continue farther south to
relocate in the Springfield vicinity.

"Bigger town," Walter Carlin said as they came to
say their good-byes, his wife and son standing nearby.
"We've got no family to go to, so Springfield seems a
better bet for us. We've got a better chance to find work
there."

"You've been good neighbors," Jacob said. "We'll miss you."

There were hugs between the mothers and handshakes between the fathers. Mitch and Bobby stood an arm's length apart, emotions tearing at them, but, fearing the appearance of softness, they merely stared and shuffled.

"Bye, Mitch," Bobby said finally. "Maybe we'll run into each other someday."

"Sure, we will," Mitch said, and he quickly turned away, afraid his friend would see the sentiment that was misting his eyes.

That very night, with Bobby waiting outside, Mitch came to his parents wearing his hat, his only warm coat, and with a few personal possessions in a sack. "We're going to find Quantrill," Mitch announced. "We're going to join up."

"You mustn't!" his mother pleaded. "You're just a child. Stay with us. . . . The war won't last."

"Bobby and I have made up our minds," he countered. "I'm not a kid anymore."

"Son, the South can't last," his father argued. "Do what your mother says—stay out of it."

Despite his mother's tears and continued pleadings, his sister's dismay, and his father's stern warnings, Mitch said his hasty good-byes and hurried to join Bobby.

On foot, the young pair walked and caught wagon rides to the gathering place. Less than a month had passed since the raid on Lawrence, and Federal troops, pouring into the region, were on the hunt for Quantrill's guerrillas. Hundreds of his men, who had scattered after the attack on the Kansas town, were converging again at the Perdee farm a short distance from the community of Lee's Summit in Missouri. Remarkably, the regrouping had been totally undetected by the roaming troops of Union soldiers.

"What do you want?" a gruff, scrawny man at the open gate of the farm challenged as they approached. He wore an oversized butternut blouse over his shirt, baggy denim trousers, and a black, low-crowned western hat with a round, wide brim. He held a shotgun at port and turned it toward the new arrivals.

Behind him, a few men in similar apparel lounged in the shade of the trees at the front of the farmhouse. At the back of the outbuildings, Mitch could see tents and wagons, horses and men, in a huge cluster of activity. A few of the men wore Confederate grays, while others, surprisingly, wore the Union blue. Most men, however, were dressed the same way as the gate guard, in garb that appeared to be some sort of a guerrilla uniform.

"We've come to join up," Bobby said boldly. "We're here to fight."

"How'd you know we was here?" the scrawny man questioned.

"Just heard it," Mitch put in. "Most border folks know."

One of the group nearby broke away and walked to

join the scrawny man and the two boys. He was a young man with tufts of blond hair spilling from beneath his hat. He directed a question at the guard. "Who are these two?"

"They ain't yet said," the scrawny man responded. "Say they want to join up."

"Robert Carlin and Mitchell Ellsworth." Bobby made the introductions. "We've walked a piece to get here."

"Why do you want to join?" the blond man asked.

"Our folks've been burned out," Bobby said. "At least, my folks."

The blond man's attention shifted to Mitch, a question in his face.

"Took over our house," Mitch explained. "Used it to quarter Union officers."

The blond man considered them and then nodded. "Sign 'em up," he said as he walked away.

"Who was that?" Mitch asked.

"George Todd," the gate guard told them.

"Seems like a nice fellow," Bobby said.

The scrawny man chuckled.

"Wish they had given us horses," Mitch complained. "'Stead of this."

The continual haze of choking dust from the many riders ahead enveloped them, making the path for their wagon almost invisible and their breathing difficult even through their bandannas. Even so, they were lucky. Their wagon and another one directly behind carried food rations, water, rifles, and ammunition. They were in the middle of a loosely regimented column of nearly four hundred men, while other, less fortunate wagon drivers at the rear of the procession faced and swallowed an even greater cloud of dust. Many of the riders, especially at the head of the column, were wearing the blues of their enemies, a camouflage to help ease them through the Union-patrolled state.

Bobby was handling the reins, while Mitch sat on the hard wooden seat next to him. A horseman appeared out of the spray of fine grit, heading for the rear of the guerrillas' southbound march. With a curious glance at the two young men in the freight wagon, he turned his horse to a walk alongside them. "You're the new boys, aren't you?"

"Yes, sir," Bobby said as he and Mitch uncovered their faces. "Proud to be with you and Colonel Quantrill."

Bill Gregg, to whose unit they were assigned, was a long-faced man in his mid twenties, appointed third lieutenant to Quantrill. By reputation he was a stalwart raider with a fervent Confederate belief and purpose. "What are you?" he asked Bobby. "Fifteen?" His eyes shifted to Mitch. "Fourteen?"

"Eighteen," Bobby declared. "He's seventeen."

Gregg smiled his disbelief. "Look, boys, I know why you joined up. What was done to your families was wicked business—ain't no doubt about that."

"We want to get into the action, not ride in a wagon eating dust," Bobby ventured, his face taut with impatience.

Gregg laughed and nodded. "You'll get your chance, sooner or later." He directed a question to Mitch. "Two of you figured to get in on the fun of shooting up them Lincoln fellers—ain't that the size of it?"

"Yes, sir, we're looking forward to doing just that," Mitch answered, finding his voice. "Could you tell us, sir, just where we might be heading?"

"I reckon you got a right to know. We're holing up down in Texas for the winter," Gregg told them. "We'll give 'em hell again come spring." He gave them a nod and wheeled his horse to move toward the rear of the column.

"That was darned nice of him, talking to us," Bobby said. "You think he'll let us meet Colonel Quantrill?"

"I'd be happy if he'd get us on horseback," Mitch replied, pulling his kerchief back up over his nose.

Before sunset the guerrilla troops bivouacked at the side of the road, individual groups building small fires for cooking and to ward off the evening chill of early October. Bobby and Mitch had parked the wagon and were soon drafted as helpers in preparing the evening meal.

On this march to warmer climes, the cooks made no effort to please the palates. The evening's food was simple fare, a concoction brewed in a kettle over a separate fire. The slumgullion featured more potatoes, onions, and water than bits of dried meat. Coffee was served in abundance, and canned peaches served as dessert.

As the half light of dusk deepened, Mitch was helping the cook clean up while Bobby was making the rounds in a circle of seventeen men with a graniteware coffeepot. One scowling man was an intimidating, grizzled figure, thick through the chest and shoulders, a vivid red scar only partially hidden under the salt-and-pepper stubble on his cheeks. As Bobby finished filling this man's mug, he moved the pot toward the next, and a small splash of the hot liquid dropped onto the burly man's hand.

"Damn you, you miserable little puke!" the man swore, and he put his lips to his hand to suck at the afflicted skin.

"Sorry," Bobby said, and he started to move on.

The man's response was quick and vicious, a mere flick of the wrist as he launched the hot coffee from his mug at the youngster's face. Bobby's reflexes were fast; he snapped his head away and turned, most of the boiling-hot liquid spattering a leg of his jeans, the rest splashing to the ground. He backed away, dividing his attention between his assailant and the discomfort of the heat seeping through his pant leg. He dropped the coffeepot and plucked the fabric away from his thigh.

"No danged call for that, Sam!" came a rumbling voice from the gathering.

"Leave the youngster alone!" came another.

"Go home and be a crybaby to your ugly old momma," the man called Sam spat at Bobby, and then he turned away. "Hey, Cookie," he called, "get me some fresh coffee!"

"Stand up," Bobby said unexpectedly.

The grizzled raider's face showed genuine surprise, then a smile that puckered his ugly scar. "Pleased to oblige," he said, and he rose, his hand moving to slide a large combat knife from a scabbard on his belt.

"The kid ain't armed!" shouted a strongly built, bearded man, who rose to his feet. "Ain't fair, Sam."

"His problem," Sam responded, his eyes fixed on his prey. He circled and kept moving forward, his knife hand waving back and forth as Bobby retreated, putting the fire between them.

"Give him a chance!" the bearded protester persisted, his deep voice demanding. "Fistfight, no knife!"

"I'll cut you next if you butt in," the aggressor said without breaking his intent gaze on Bobby. "Stay outta this."

All the men were standing now, displaying excitement and nervous laughter, most apparently pleased, seeing entertainment in the confrontation.

Bobby moved warily, keeping the campfire between him and his assailant. The belligerent man moved in a crouch, with quick feints to one side of the fire and then a dash to the other. Bobby was as quick on his feet to avoid each charge, but his knife-wielding adversary appeared to be a skilled close-combat fighter and most likely would soon prevail.

The brawny, bearded dissenter stepped out from the crowd, grim-faced, ready to intervene, then paused with a slight smile. No one else noticed Mitch coming from the back of the nearby wagon until he swung the frying pan. The blow came down hard on the cutthroat's hat and staggered him. As he turned with glazed eyes and a gaping mouth, Mitch brought the frying pan around again and slammed it onto the crumpled hat crown. The hat flew off, and the bully sagged, the knife falling from his hand. He fell face-first into the dirt, his hair only inches from the fire. With a calm demeanor, Mitch dropped the frying pan, bent down to grab both boots of the inert raider, pulled him away from the flames, then patted the thick hair that was beginning to smolder.

"That ain't fair!" shouted an angry onlooker, who charged forward. "Two against one!"

"Shut up," came a new voice. The blond-haired man they'd met upon their arrival at the farm stepped into the firelight. "I saw the end of it," George Todd said to the crowd. "I don't need any stupid fights among our men." He turned to Bobby. "You start this?"

"In a way, I guess," Bobby answered.

"What way?"

"I dripped a little coffee on him by accident, and he got mad about it," Bobby said.

Todd turned to a knot of nearby men. "Is that all there was to it?"

"Sam tried to throw hot coffee into the kid's face," one of the men said. "And he said something nasty about the kid's momma."

On the ground, the injured man was stirring, raising his hands to his head, groaning.

Todd swept his gaze across the gathering and returned

it to Bobby and Mitch, who had moved close together. "You boys want to do some fighting, we'll give you plenty." He searched the surrounding group. "Wilson, find a couple of nags for these gamecocks, and get 'em outfitted." He returned his attention to the young pair. "You have your own weapons?

Both nodded.

"Pick that man up and stick him in one of the wagons," Todd instructed no one in particular. "If his head ain't busted, he'll report for duty in the morning, sure as any other."

As two men lifted the ruffian to his feet and half walked, half dragged him from the gathering, the fair-fight advocate approached Mitch and Bobby. "I'm Luke McGrath," he introduced himself. "You watch out for Sam, young fellers," he said in a somber tone. "He'll stew on this for a long time, and, I reckon, he'll figger to do you some hurt." As he walked away, he warned, "Keep your eyes peeled."

Chapter Six

Shortly after sunup, the boy, Andy, came into the room with a clean denim shirt on a hanger, carrying Mitch's hat, vest, trousers, and boots as well. "Ma said to give you this," he said, indicating the shirt. "It was my pa's. Yours was all bloody."

Mitch rose slowly and painfully, then reached for the articles of clothing and laid them on the divan. "What happened to your pa?"

Susan Jennings entered the room with a large gunnysack in her hands. "I've got extra bandages, cotton, and a bottle of iodine in here. You've got to keep that wound clean and not let it get infected." She paused. "There's a near pint of whiskey in there too. You can drink it if you must, but it would be better used to boil the heat out of that sore spot." Again she hesitated. "There's also a bottle of laudanum solution in there for the pain. No more *ever* than thirty drops—that would be two capfuls. Try not to use it more than you have to. It'll dope you up pretty good."

Mitch reached for the sack and regarded it. "Laudanum?"

"The doctor gave me some, and you've been getting your share over the past few days," she told him. Then she added, "Will, my husband, came home from the war with two Confederate bullets still in him, bullets the surgeons couldn't reach," she said. "For a while it was all right: they didn't seem to bother him." She took a ragged breath. "Then the one near his spine moved closer, and the pain came. In the end, laudanum was the only thing that kept him from screaming night and day." She took a long breath. "My husband died before using up the bottle I'm giving you."

They stood silently for a moment.

"Go on outside, Andy, and bring his horse," she told her son. After he ran from the room, she turned again to Mitch. "Get dressed. Your mare's been rested and fed, and I saddled her at first light."

Mitch glanced at the chain binding him to the divan.

She handed him a key. She stepped out of the room and immediately returned, a Navy Colt in her hand. "I'll be right outside while you dress." She nodded at the revolver. "I'm good with it."

He nodded.

"You'll have to go without your pistol. I'm keeping

it," she told him. "I won't have it on my conscience for somebody to be killed because I helped you."

"I understand," he said.

She stepped out of the room.

Mitch inserted the key into the manacle, unsnapped the cuff from his wrist, and then unfastened the remaining cuff from the leg of the divan. He dropped the manacle and slowly, painfully, put on the shirt and the trousers. Pulling on socks and boots was hardest, the strain on the injured muscles flaring into agony. Finally finished, he rose and put on his vest and his hat. He glanced at the manacle he'd dropped. "Might come in right handy," he murmured to himself. To avoid making noise, he carefully lifted the manacle and put it into the bag. Moments later he walked unsteadily into the main room of the house.

The woman reached toward him, but he waved her away. "Be wise not to get close, ma'am," he said with a hint of sarcasm. "I can make it."

"Point taken," she replied with muted mockery of her own.

Mitch walked slowly to the front door, opened it, and stepped outside. The early-summer morning was cool, and a slight breeze felt good. He crossed the porch and carefully descended the two steps to the flagstone walk, then made his way to the hitching rail, where the boy stood with his horse. He draped the gunnysack over his saddle, tied it to the saddle horn, and then looked down at the stirrup.

"Can you get up on her, mister?" the youngster asked.

"I can," Mitch replied, reaching for the saddle horn with his left hand.

"Step away from him, Andy," the woman commanded.

"He's hurt, Ma," the boy responded.

"He'll be all right. Leave him alone."

The boy handed the reins to Mitch and stepped away with obvious reluctance. "Hope you'll be better soon, mister!"

Mitch nodded and lifted his left leg high to insert his foot into the stirrup. Using mainly the strength of his left arm, he pulled himself up, feeling a surge of pain coursing through his torso from the wound. The throbbing eased as he swung into the saddle, and he rested, feeling a sudden sweat beading his brow.

"Are you all right?" the woman asked anxiously.

Mitch unbuttoned his shirt. He pulled it away from his body and peered at the bandage inside. "Looks okay," he said as he re-buttoned it. "Nothing pulled loose."

The woman moved to the side of the horse. "Go as far as you can, and find someplace to rest. Good luck to you."

"You've been kind, ma'am. I won't forget what you've done."

"Get lost, Mitchell Ellsworth," she admonished him. "Get away as far as you can. Put all this behind you, and try to be a decent man."

"I can't rightly forget what's happened hereabouts,"

Mitch responded with solemnity. "About the men who robbed the bank—did Carlin get away?" he asked.

The woman regarded him with a look of scorn. "You're going after him, aren't you?"

· Mitch didn't answer.

"Are you going to kill him?"

Mitch touched the brim of his hat in a salute of thanks and, with a slight tug on the reins, turned the horse and urged it into a gentle walk. He glanced toward the back of the property and could see freshly turned earth in the burial plot. *It would be bad for the woman should the empty grave be opened,* he reflected. *Very bad.* He shifted in the saddle, leaning to his left to lessen the effect of the jarring motion, and booted the mare into a trot, gritting his teeth against the pain. When he was out of sight of the house, he reined the mare back into an easy, rhythmic gait.

He headed south rather than returning to the Lebanon vicinity. *Should the marshal of Mayfield discover the burial ruse,* he considered, *a manhunt would focus on his home base.*

A second and more important reason for taking this direction was his sense that he could follow Bob Carlin's path to his hideout. The gently rolling hills and level lands he now traveled encompassed much of the southern section of Missouri. Farther south, in the Arkansas Ozarks, the hills became steeper, round-topped, verdant mountains with deep, lush valleys between them. In that densely wooded, wild, and rugged territory, clannish people had made their isolated homesteads, suspicious of outsiders and often even their own neighbors. However, many of these hill people had roots in the southlands and, during the war and after, could occasionally be persuaded or bribed into providing a haven for those at odds with the law.

That's where we hid before, Mitch reflected. "My guess is, that's where he'll go now," he said aloud.

He stiffened his resolve against the pain and rode through the morning and late into the afternoon. He was determined to put himself a far distance from Mayfield and the woman's farm. This Ozark plateau had been settled by farmers, houses and barns built, and the land cleared for fenced pastures. Small villages and towns had been established and were growing. Roads such as the one he traveled had become busy thoroughfares of commerce. Twice during his ride he rode Belle to small streams to let her drink her fill and to give her and his side a chance to rest.

The slant of the afternoon sun told him the time was about five o'clock. Pain-plagued, saddle-sore, and exhausted, he considered and relished the thought of a comfortable hotel bed in the next Missouri town. He immediately dismissed the notion with the cold realization that he, with an ashen face and the appearance of a gunshot wound, would be subject to unwanted scrutiny.

A June night outdoors should be warm enough.

The stand of mixed woods—pinion oaks and pines— was substantial, a half-acre or more surrounded by pastureland. The strands of barbed wire fencing that marked the land's ownership were high in some places, while other sections lay flat on the ground between weathered posts. Mitch guided his mare through such a fence break into the welcome cool of the woodland shadows. Sunlight danced through the overhead canopy of breeze-fluttered leaves, the cool location would provide a refuge from the outside world.

He walked the mare a distance from the road and found a clearing. No stream for fresh water ran though the grove, but there was enough left in the canteen the Jennings woman had thoughtfully filled. He dismounted slowly and looked for a place to rest. His side burned, and he was loath to examine the wound, afraid of what he would find.

He tied the reins to the slender trunk of a young tree and ignored the head turns of his mare. The horse, impatient for the saddle to be removed, nipped at him, and he boxed her nose away. "Sorry, lass," he said sympathetically. "No strength to take it off, and, Lord knows, I'd never be able to get it on your back again and cinch those straps."

He untied and removed the gunnysack. He took out the manacle and tucked it into one of his saddlebags. To his surprise, he found that the woman had packed him a cheese sandwich in waxed paper and an apple. He rummaged farther and discovered his revolver and cartridge belt at the bottom. "Thank you, ma'am," he said aloud. "Promise not to shoot nobody 'less I have to." He stood by the horse and ate the sandwich, then fed the apple to the eager mare. He unfastened his bedroll from the behind the saddle, untied the gunnysack, and carried both as he looked for a smooth spot on the ground.

He brushed away the crinkly dried leaves of previous falls and winters and found a soft green growth of grass beneath. Moving sluggishly, he undid his bedroll and sat down heavily with a great sigh. He remained motionless for several minutes, the exertions of the past few minutes exhausting. At last he unbuttoned his shirt and slowly, painfully, struggled out of it. He laid it aside and looked down at his bandage. He noted with concern a bit of blood seepage and, with deliberation, removed the gauze and plaster. With his torso bare, he examined the wound and was gratified to see that it was no longer weeping blood, the flesh sewn securely. About the line of incision, a dull red flush on either side seemed of minor concern. No threads of infection branched out from the lesion, and he breathed a sigh of relief and thanksgiving. Nonetheless, he took the bottle of whiskey from the sack and dripped it over the wound. He gritted his teeth as it stung the incision, and he comforted himself that the infection was slight. Clumsily he dabbed iodine on it, then bandaged himself once again and donned his shirt. He administered the laudanum sparingly and put the medical materials aside. He squirmed into a supine position placed his hands over his eyes to shut out the daylight. He lay listening to the soft rustle of the slight breeze through the trees, the distant cry of birds, the chattering of a squirrel somewhere nearby in the woods. He felt the laudanum overwhelming his senses and gratefully welcomed the bliss of diminishing pain. A few moments later the opiate enveloped him in wild imaginings and then faded his dreams into a restful and untroubled sleep.

Chapter Seven

Consciousness returned in the wee, dark hours of the next morning. Awareness had crept back gradually, barely there at first to register the nocturnal sounds of the woodland. He could hear his mare nearby, grazing on the grass and, occasionally, the nighttime foraging of small animals. Drowsily he fought the arrival of awareness, wanting to linger in the comfort of the drug and fearful of a renewal of pain. But pain in his side prevailed and brought his mind to a sharp alertness. He sat up with effort and was somewhat pleased to feel a bit of new strength. The wound still throbbed, but it seemed slightly less agonizing now. For the first time since being shot, he felt he was regaining strength and well-being.

A cool, light wind relieved the sultry air and brought a nickering from his mare. She was aware that he was awake and registered her displeasure at the nightlong weight of the saddle and the lack of feed and care.

"Sorry, girl," he said in a low voice. "You've had plenty of grass here. It'll have to do."

He considered the possibility of more sleep but knew that wouldn't happen. He was wide awake, his mind racing with the dangers behind and ahead of him.

He rose to a squatting position, then rerolled his bedding. Rising stiffly, gingerly, he walked to his horse and, in pain, repositioned the bedroll behind the saddle. He looked through the other pocket of the saddlebag and found, to his great satisfaction, that the woman had also left a half loaf of bread and some beef jerky, each wrapped in butcher's paper. Not a customary breakfast, but one he munched in appreciation.

He unfastened the reins and, favoring his right side, struggled to mount his mare. Close to a swoon, he rested astride the saddle until his faintness subsided and his strength revived. He nudged the sides of his horse and turned her back toward the road.

The night was clear, starlight dimly illuminating the road as he guided his mare out of the woods and headed her south. Even though he, Mitchell Ellsworth, was now reported dead and buried, he was still concerned that he might be mistaken for one of the other Harrisonville bank robbers. He considered a plan to stay on the road when it appeared empty and to keep a watchful eye out for places of concealment, should he need to leave it. His horse moved at a steady pace, the rocking motion bringing him once again to near somnolence. Time passed in which he drowsed, came alert, and then dozed again.

As dawn erased the night sky, Mitch forced himself to a mental state of wariness. He scanned the distant road and looked to his right and to his left at the few farmhouses he passed, noting that lamps were shining in the windows. At a few of faraway farm dwellings, he could see figures moving in the yards or near the barns.

He was familiar with this section of the state from travels long ago. He was moving south parallel to the Missouri–Kansas border. The Arkansas line was still a considerable distance away, and there were a number of towns along the way.

As the sun rose above the horizon, traffic on the road increased. To the travelers he met or passed, he gave friendly waves, and, without exception, the responses were jovial "Howdys" and "Good mornings." The volume of traffic on the road cheered him as he reconsidered his earlier plan to travel evasively. With many people on the road, he had a better chance of mingling with them without being stopped or questioned.

He came up behind a slow-moving van drawn by a single horse. As he rode nearer, he recalled that he had seen it before. In the haze of his memory and his befuddled awakening in Mayfield, he vaguely recalled that the same van had been in the back of the crowd while the man with the camera was taking his picture. Moving his horse to its side, he could now see and remember the flowing script on the dark wood—JONATHAN PEABODY, FRONTIER PHOTOGRAPHER.

As Mitch's horse moved alongside the front of the wagon, a young, bearded man in the driver's seat gave him a wary glance and then lifted one hand in a hesitant salute.

Mitch returned the gesture and manufactured a friendly manner. "Good day to you."

"And the same to you, sir," the young man responded, his hands working the reins to guide the horse to the most even sections of the dirt road. "Not in your way, am I?"

"Not at all," Mitch answered, and he moved his mare closer to the wagon. "Mr. Peabody . . . photographer fellow, are you? I've seen you before."

"That so? Whereabouts?"

"Mayfield. Some number of days ago."

The young man risked taking his eyes from the road to look at Mitch. "I was there, all right."

Doesn't recognize me, Mitch thought with satisfaction, his hand touching the stubble of his new beard. "You were taking pictures of those dead men."

The young man was still on guard. "Meant them no disrespect," he said.

"What was the picture for?"

"Historic journals, that sort of thing," Peabody said, a trifle too quickly.

"Newspapers?"

"Possibly."

"Possibly?"

"More than likely," Peabody admitted. "You're not kin or a close friend, are you?"

Mitch shook his head. "Just curious, that's all."

"Well, I'm moving pretty slowly. Don't want to hold you up."

"If you don't mind, I'll just ride along with you for a spell," Mitch told him. "We can talk a bit to pass the time."

"I guess that would be all right," Peabody conceded.

"This rig of yours," Mitch asked as he looked at the enclosed wagon, "is that where you . . . what do you call it?"

"Develop the pictures? That's right."

"Interesting," Mitch said. "Saw some of those pictures by that Brady fellow about the war."

"Matthew Brady," Peabody acknowledged. "I'm not in his class, but I do what I can."

"Those two fellows there in Mayfield," Mitch said. "Word was that one of 'em wasn't dead yet. That bother you, taking his likeness before he was cold?"

"They said he was a goner," the young man said defensively. "Those two were nothing but outlaws, killers who had no mercy."

"That what they were?"

Peabody gave an emphatic nod. "Scalawags, both of 'em."

"What are you looking for next?" Mitch asked.

"Heard there might be some subjects of interest down

here in the south country," Peabody responded. "Aim to find out if there's any shooting going on." He nodded. "Might make for some interesting pictures."

Mitch rode in silence for a couple of minutes, then leaned out to speak. "I'd best be moving on. Been interesting talking to you."

"My pleasure, sir. I didn't catch your name."

Mitch urged his horse into a trot without giving an answer. "*I'm* a scalawag?" he muttered, reining his mare to a slower gait a hundred feet ahead of the photographer's van. He touched his right side with his palm as if the warmth of his hand would ease the throbbing the trot had caused. He looked back at the wagon. "Maybe I just met one worse than me."

As he traveled on, he considered the possibility of finding shelter for the night. He still felt the need for a deep sleep of recuperation and decided to chance a room and a bed. He was north of the Missouri town of Nevada and decided to ride down a side road to seek a lesser settlement, where lawmen would be few if any.

A few miles closer to the Kansas line, he rode into a tiny village with only five commercial buildings and fewer than a dozen houses. He reined his mare to a halt and raised a hand to attract the attention of one of the three men he saw walking along the central street. "May I ask you a question, sir?"

The three men stopped walking as one. A portly fellow in bib overalls raised his straw-hatted head to regard the stranger. "Do what I can if I know the answer," he said with a cheerful expression on his weathered face.

"Anyplace here where I can get a room, a place to get some sleep?"

The farmer shrugged. "Might ride on into the next town. They got a hotel there."

"I'm tired and worn out here and now," Mitch responded.

"Might try the third house up there," the man said, turning to point. "Bert and Vera Wommack got a room they let out. If they got somebody full-time, you're outta luck."

"Thanks, I'll give 'em a try," Mitch said with a nod of thanks as he started his horse forward.

"Nice room!" the farmer called. "Won't cost you a bunch."

Mitch waved and rode his mare toward the designated house. It was a large, rambling structure, all on the ground level, a white-painted clapboard house onto which a couple of extra rooms had been oddly and lopsidedly attached. Behind the house he could see a shed, a small barn, and an outhouse.

He dismounted slowly, stiffly, and tied the reins of his horse to the hitching rail at the edge of the fenceless yard. He opened a flap of his saddlebags and searched for and found his small leather money bag. He hefted it a couple of times to judge the contents, shook his head, and put it into an inside pocket of his vest. With some misgivings about his haggard appearance, he walked to the front porch and up the steps of to the door. He rapped three times, waited, and was about to rap again when an elderly man appeared, peering through the screen.

"Mr. Wommack? I'm told you have a room to rent out?" Mitch said as a question.

The old man looked him up and down. "How long you planning to stay?"

"A night, maybe two."

The old man shook his head. "Three nights or she's a no-go. Cost you six bits each night." He looked closely at Mitch's face. "Cash in advance, but you get a good breakfast every day."

"What about my horse?"

"Barn in the back. Costs four bits extra for feed."

"Each day?"

"No, sir. One-time fee, that's all."

Mitch nodded, took the pouch from his vest pocket, opened it, and counted out coins for the proper total.

"Bed sleeps good," the old man said, counting the coins for himself. "The old lady don't allow no bedbugs or lice on the folks what stays." He cocked his head. "You clean?"

Mitch nodded. "Trail dust and summer sweat, that's all."

"Well, the old lady don't have to look at you in the raw, but she will want to check your clothes before you lie down. Deal's off if there's any cooties jumping around. That all right with you?"

"Have to be, I guess," Mitch said. "I'll take my horse out to the barn."

"Come in the back door when you're through," the old man instructed. "The old lady will have some coffee for you or maybe a drink of whiskey if you'd rather. No extra charge."

"Thanks," Mitch said as he turned toward his horse. "Some cool water, and then I'm straight for some bed rest."

"You ain't sick, are you?"

"No, just bone tired."

Mitch walked to the hitching rail, untied the reins, and walked the mare around the side of the house to the barn. An old, forlorn horse stood in one of three stalls, her matted coat showing a lack of grooming. Mitch led Belle into the third stall. With grimaces and grunts of pain, he unfastened the straps and slid, rather than lifted, the heavy saddle from the mare's back. He propped the saddle against a wall to allow the underside of it to dry, then turned to stroke the animal's neck and withers. "Maybe I can rub you down tomorrow," he told her. "When, maybe, I'll be up to it." He forked some hay into the stall, poured a modest amount of rolled oats into a feeding trough, then bid the horse a good evening and walked out of the barn.

He held himself straight and forced what he hoped appeared to be a normal, uninjured gait to the back door of the house. He opened the screen door and stepped into the kitchen, where an elderly woman was waiting. She was a half head taller than her husband, who stood in a doorway to a different part of the house. Her white hair was tousled, and her face was raddled with age. She looked to be in her nineties, with the loss of most of her teeth creating sunken cheeks and a pinched mouth.

"Good afternoon," Mitch said to her.

"Going right to bed?" she asked.

"Soon," he replied.

"Something to eat?"

He shook his head. "Tomorrow's soon enough."

She handed him a glass of water and watched while he drank it down. "More?"

"No, thank you," he replied, and he handed back the glass. "That was just fine."

With a tilt of her head, she indicated her husband. "Bert will show you the room. When you get ready for bed, lay them clothes outside the door. Your underclothes too."

Mitch nodded.

"I'll wash 'em for you if you like."

"I'll pay you," Mitch agreed.

"No need. Stick 'em in with Bert's."

"Thank you. I'd appreciate it."

"Ain't got a tub," she went on. "They do baths down at the barbershop if you want."

"Not a bad idea," Mitch responded.

The woman turned abruptly and pointed to her husband. "Go along with Bert."

Mitch gave her another nod and followed the old man, who led him down a dark hallway to a door. The old man opened it and stepped aside to allow Mitch to enter.

The small, austere room was a surprise. Wallpapered

in a subdued, vertically striped floral pattern, it was neat and well tended. A window with its shade half-open brought a sunny cheer to the chamber. A brass double bed with a clean, colorful quilt occupied most of the space. A gray graniteware washbasin and pitcher sat atop a small table under a mirror and towel rack. On a bedside table a well-worn, leather-bound Bible was significantly displayed.

"There's fresh water in the pitcher," the old man said. He nodded to a towel and washcloth on the rod over the table. "You might want to sponge off some of your trail dust." He turned and left the room, closing the door behind him.

Mitch laid his saddlebags and the gunnysack at the foot of the bed and stepped to the window. He could see most of the main street and the handful of buildings that made up the rural community. In the reddish light of late afternoon, it resembled a still-life painting, with only a lone pedestrian and a horse-drawn wagon to mar the illusion. He fingered the money pouch in his pocket and worried about how little was left, with no way to withdraw more of his meager savings from his distant bank. His remaining funds amounted to seven dollars and a few pennies. Enough for some food, he reflected, but nothing to keep him in the comfort of a real bed under a roof for long. Worse, he was physically unfit even to do a day's work to earn a penny or two more.

He drew down the shade, and dejection descended as well. In the russet gloom he pulled back the bed's quilt and top sheet and began to undress. He stripped and folded his clothing. Naked, he carefully removed the bandage from his side and inspected the wound. Although some small bloodstains had dried on the dressing and around the stitched cut, the wound showed no further signs of oozing. He poured water into the washbasin and dipped the washcloth into it repeatedly, washing his face, hands, and torso. He bathed the skin around the incision with care and toweled himself dry. He hid the old dressing and rebandaged the wound.

With caution he partially opened the bedroom door, glanced around to make sure the hallway was empty, and placed his folded clothing outside. He closed the door, moved to the bed, and pondered a dose of laudanum. *Don't need it,* he decided. He slipped into the bed and lay on his good side to await the healing blessing of sleep.

He didn't wait long.

Chapter Eight

On the third morning, after a full and satisfying breakfast, Mitch thanked his elderly hosts and carried his be-
longings to the barn. Despite the pain of the exertion, he
found the strength to hoist the saddle onto the mare and
pull the cinch straps tight. He led the horse outside and
delighted in his renewed energy as he stepped into the stirrup and swung up to sit in the saddle. He guided the horse
out to the road and, in under five minutes, put the tiny village behind him.

Heading south once more, he marveled at the differ-
ence a bath and a couple of days' rest had made. Though
not yet fully recovered, he did have an evolving sense
of well-being. The pain of his wound was dull now, sharp
only when a straining movement aggravated it.

The morning was bright and clear with no signs of

clouds on the horizon. His mare was frisky, perhaps in an animal empathy with his own elevated spirits. He had visited the barn yesterday for a belated grooming session, and, although he had managed only a feeble effort, the mare seemed comfortable with it.

North of Joplin, he cut away from the main road and found alternate trails to circle around the community. On the other side of the town he came back to the major southbound lane and continued his journey toward Arkansas. He had traveled this part of southwest Missouri for the first time long ago. He remembered the day, recalling Bobby as his equally callow companion and those new, tough comrades, good and bad, who had ridden with them.

In early October of 1863, the guerrillas crossed over into Kansas only a few miles north of the Indian Territory. Although Quantrill's army was generally favored with good, spirited horses, Mitch and Bobby sat astride a couple of steeds far more suited for the slaughterhouse than combat. By the sluggish pace of their animals, they were relegated to the rear of the moving column.

At midmorning there was a flurry of activity at the front of the line, and the procession came to a stop. There was much wonderment and speculation, riders fanning out on either side of the road, trying to determine the cause of the standstill. Finally a horseman rode down the sprawling line, stopping at intervals for brief conversations. When he finally approached the last assemblage, the men crowded around on foot and on horseback, eager to listen.

"Davey Pool and his advance boys caught a couple of fellers on a lumber wagon heading to deliver a load to a little ol' Yankee fort they got up there," the bearer of news said. "Them fellers said that there's maybe less than a hundred or so troops there, a whole bunch of them Negro fellers wearing blue soldier coats."

"A fort?" one of the listeners questioned.

"Ain't much of one," came the answer. "Some cabins, tents, and a waist-high wall is about all they got. And looks like one whole side of that wall ain't even there yet."

"What we planning to do about that?" another voice asked.

"The colonel's got Bill Gregg heading up a bunch of us to take 'em out," the messenger told them. "Looks like we're gonna have us some fun."

In the next fifteen minutes Mitch and Bobby were ordered into a detachment to raid the small garrison. Their sizable guerrilla party covered the short distance and, at high noon, arrived at the crude facility. It was a rudimentary installation with cabins both inside and outside an enclosure of log-strengthened earthen embankments only four feet high. The fourth of these barricade walls was missing, leaving a wide-open vulnerability.

The assault was a surprise to the men in the camp. Many of the black soldiers were at a cooking site yards away from the three-sided embankment, and few had weapons with them. As the horseback raiders came in screaming and yelling, pistols firing, pandemonium ensued. Some of the Union soldiers scattered and ran into the brush, while others were cut down as they dashed for the cover of the log-and-dirt barricade. Surprisingly, most of the pursued made it to the scant safety of the fort walls, the shouting raiders right behind them. A couple of the guerrilla riders jumped their steeds over the embankment, wheeling their mounts and nearly trampling their frantic prey.

Mitch dug his heels hard into the sides of his mare and bent low over the neck, an old Navy Colt in his right hand. The bay responded with a loping, labored gallop into the midst of battle. Out of the corner of his eye he saw Bobby veering his horse into the surrounding woods in pursuit of a fleeing Union soldier. Mitch's attention switched immediately to one of the few white Federal troops, a young officer in the western breach of the embankment, shouting orders and urging his troops to withstand the rebels' onslaught. Mitch turned his horse toward the officer, hoping to gun down this person in command. A shot whizzed by his ear, and the closeness of the miss both scared and puzzled him. *Bluebelly behind him?*

Suddenly his mare stumbled, front legs buckling, plunging toward the barren earth. Mitch tried to leap free but was slammed to the ground, his left leg hammered by the weight of the fallen horse. The impact to his upper body brought instant pain, but the leg was without feeling, as numb as if it didn't exist at all.

Mitch curled his aching torso against the lifeless mare as other horses' hooves trampled dangerously about him. He summoned his will for survival and struggled again and again to pull his leg free. With a grim sense of futility, he gave up the effort for the moment, waiting for strength, praying for help to arrive.

A horse came close and stopped, and a large man leaped down from the saddle. "Hang on, boy. I'll getcha out."

Mitch recognized Luke McGrath as the same bearded man who had stepped forward and protested the unfair fight two nights before.

The big man reached for the saddle horn on the back of the dead mare and, straining every muscle of his legs and substantial torso, used it to lever the weight a scant few inches higher. "Do 'er now!" he shouted.

Mitch placed both hands behind him on the ground and his right foot against the horse and shoved as hard as he was able.

The leg came free!

"Stay down!" the man commanded, and he remounted his horse. "I'll be back fer ya."

Mitch lay behind the dead animal, using it as a shield from the rifle and pistol fire coming from the fort. The pain of his fall was subsiding to soreness, and some feeling was returning to his leg. Head down, he reached toward his tingling thigh and felt the knee and calf. Nothing seemed broken, and there was no sign of blood seeping through his jeans. Despite the pins-and-needles stings, he flexed the leg and took great satisfaction that no permanent damage seemed to have been done. He reached toward his holster and then realized that his Navy Colt had flown from his hand during his fall. He shrugged and accepted the role of a noncombatant.

Mitch peered over the carcass to gauge the situation of the battle. His fellow raiders were milling about on their horses, charging and wheeling in the melee, a churning, violent scene of shots being fired yet with seemingly few hits. A new sound thundered, and a shell arced high and exploded harmlessly in the woods. Even so, there was a marked effect upon the attacking force; the charging horses were reined to a stop, and confusion held sway.

"They got a howitzer, boys!" someone shouted. "Back off! Back off!"

Almost meekly the raiders turned in retreat, a few firing shots over their shoulders at the fort, although many appeared to have simply lost interest. At the fortification, both black and white soldiers were rising and clapping their hands in celebration. Mitch watched with dismay and a degree of disgust that this first battle was so easily abandoned by his new comrades. He tried to rise and found it difficult, his leg still a problem.

From the woods he saw Bobby emerge on horseback to join the retreat, his manner one of excitement and high spirits. Mitch stood to full height despite sporadic gunfire from the fort and waved both hands, signaling for his friend's attention. Bobby continued to ride along with two other men as they moved away.

Didn't he see me?

Luke McGrath rode to Mitch and reined his mount to a stop, removing his boot from his left stirrup, "Jump up 'hind me!"

Mitch reached for the saddle horn and tried to lift his numb left leg to the stirrup, then shook his head. "Can't make it," he said despondently.

"Hang on, then," McGrath instructed.

Mitch tightened his grip on the saddle horn and dangled at the side as the man kicked the horse to a trot. It took all of his strength to hold on as the horse carried him and its rider away from the battlefield. Several times his feet touched and bounced against the ground, and several times he felt his fingers slipping. Once, when his grip truly slipped, the rider reached down at the last possible moment and pulled him up to regain his hold. Finally, at a safe distance from gunfire, his rescuer reined the horse to a stop, and Mitch crumpled to the ground.

"Okay, boy?" McGrath asked as he dismounted and stooped down to observe him.

"I think so," Mitch replied. "Nothing's broken. Just took a bad fall, and my leg's still trying to wake up."

The big man laughed. "Warn't much of a fight, what we did, were it?"

Mitch joined McGrath's laughter. "I didn't see much of it from under my horse."

"Rest up 'til you can swing up, and we'll scoot back to the outfit."

"I owe you," Mitch said, rubbing his leg, trying to coax it back to life. "I'm about ready."

"When we get there," McGrath said, his manner turning serious, "keep a close eye on old frying-pan Sam. He was shooting from your backside," McGrath told him. "I'm a-thinking he shot that nag out from under ya, but he was really aiming at *you*."

"Well, I'll be damned!" Mitch swore in dismay.

McGrath nodded. "He gets along with the colonel and the other head men—he's rode with 'em a long time. You and your pal oughta winter somewhere's else than Texas." He nodded again sagely. "If he don't get you on the road, he'll try 'er again down south."

"Where should we go?"

"I got a place down in Arkansas where you can hole up."

"Arkansas?" Mitch questioned. "Since we joined, shouldn't we stay with the main bunch?"

"Come spring, they'll be a-calling," the big man told him. "Maybe laying off this winter might mellow Sam out." He paused, then grinned. "Knowing Sam, some feller that's meaner just might kill him 'fore you ever see him again."

"That'd be a shame," Mitch responded with a shy smile.

Laughing, McGrath removed his foot from the stirrup and reached down to Mitch.

With his left leg only half willing to oblige, Mitch labored to swing up onto the saddle. McGrath nudged his horse into a walk and then prodded the steed into a trot.

The skirmish against the crude fort had been ignobly lost, a slipshod assault. Mitch didn't know about the second battle that day until it was over and done.

Quantrill, with the remainder of his troops, had been circling around to the north to aid in the attack on the fort, and on the Texas Road they ran right into a Union wagon convoy headed by Major General James Blunt. This inept commander, mistaking from a distance the oncoming raiders as Union troops from the fort, led well over one hundred men into a massacre. His Army contingent, including band members actually playing instruments in their wagon, was completely surprised. When the guerrillas charged, the Union soldiers bolted, fleeing in panic, only to be cut down in what turned out to be a slaughter. Only a few, including General Blunt, managed to escape.

That night, even though a rowdy celebration of the victory was in full swing, Mitch made his decision to split from the Texas-bound irregulars and accompany his older benefactor, Luke McGrath, to a safe haven in the densely forested Pea Ridge wilds of Arkansas north of Fayetteville. He assumed his boyhood friend would come along.

"Nope, not me," Bobby had said with an air of disdain.

"You're going on to Texas?" Mitch voiced his surprise. "You're not sticking with me?"

"I joined up with this outfit," Bobby replied. "I'm not going to spend the war hiding out with a bunch of hillbillies."

Mitch cast a mortified glance at the large man standing a few feet away. Whether McGrath heard or not, there was no indication. "For crying out loud," Mitch said in a whisper, "Luke McGrath is our friend. He stuck up for you, and he danged near saved my life."

Bobby shrugged. "I'm staying with the main outfit. I want to see some of the high times down there in Texas. You should come along too."

"You're being a fool," Mitch admonished his friend. "Come on, we're in this together."

The argument went on for a few more minutes, but at last they parted, Mitch joining Luke McGrath to head to Arkansas and Bobby on his way to Texas.

More than twenty years ago, Mitch reflected as he retraced this southern journey. Bobby had eventually come to Arkansas; he came to hide. Now was a new time, but Carlin might well come to an old hiding place that no one other than Mitchell Ellsworth would know about.

Mitch smiled.

And Mitchell Ellsworth was dead.

Chapter Nine

Almost two weeks had passed since Mitch set forth on this trail, and with warm, fair weather prevailing, he had spent the nights off the road in relative comfort. In the dark at rest or during the daytime in the saddle, he found his thoughts gathered into a nearly solitary issue: what to do about his former friend and companion. The Jennings woman had guessed right: killing would fulfill his initial fury. But reason was now persuasively replacing that rage. The penalty for committing a premeditated killing, however appropriate an end for Bob Carlin, would mean prison once again, and that would be punishment for him. On the other hand, the sentence for the robbery and killing at Harrisonville would be either hanging or, more likely, a long, long imprisonment for *Captain* Bob.

It would take away what was left of his youth and much of his middle age at the least, Mitch thought with bitter satisfaction.

Two days ago he had discarded his last wound dressing and felt reasonably optimistic about the healing despite the ugly appearance of the scarred flesh. He felt no further need for the small doses of laudanum, but he continued to doctor the wound with splashes of whiskey and dabs of iodine.

This morning, finally in Arkansas, Mitch turned from a narrow lane into a rugged, wheel-rutted track winding through the low mountains and deep valleys. He entered a forest, its leafy covering providing a gloomy shade, the atmosphere already thick and steamy with summer heat. He leaned forward in the saddle to better survey the uneven road with its protruding stones and hollow ruts. He trusted the instincts of his mount to pick her way over the treacherous ground, but a misstep of one hoof might cause him a disastrous tumble.

Mitch followed the torturous trail for a little more than four miles until he came to the edge of a small clearing. He reined his mare to a stop and turned her into the murky green tangle of the surrounding forest, not intending to show himself yet. He dismounted from his horse and tied her several yards back in the woods, then returned and moved into a thick knot of underbrush. From his hidden vantage point in the dense woods, he surveyed the log cabin, corral, and outbuildings in the center of the clearing. *Luke McGrath's place,* he considered. *Not a likely refuge for Bob Carlin and his bunch, but it might not be with the McGraths' consent.*

A wispy plume of white smoke rose from the cabin chimney to indicate cooking—certainly not heating in this steamy, sultry air. Two horses stood in the corral next to the barn a scant few yards behind the house. Tethered by a long rope, a tawny dog lay sleeping at a back corner of the cabin.

Mitch watched the backwoods dwelling for a considerable time. A tall, thin woman wearing a gray wrapper came into view to toss something to the dog and then moved out sight as the mongrel hungrily attacked his prize.

Mitch had come to know the hill folks in these mountains quite well during and after the war.

Mostly of Irish and Scottish descent, they had a fierce and independent nature. They prized their isolated way of life, settled their own quarrels, and seldom welcomed those from outside their cloistered communities. On their Ozark properties they fed themselves with vegetables from their gardens, wild fruits, milk from their cows, and meat from their chickens, their pigs, and the small forest animals they hunted. Many were southerners at heart and, during and after the Civil War, remained loyal to the precepts of the Confederacy.

"You running from the law or just come to pay a visit?" a husky voice asked from behind him.

Mitch pivoted slowly toward a brawny man with a

full beard and a wild mane of gray-flecked black hair standing ten feet behind him, a Sharps rifle at the ready in his big hands. "Good day to you, Luke," Mitch said easily. "Where's Patrick?"

"Over on your left," the big man said with equal calm. "Look close. You'll maybe see his rifle pointing at ya."

"Howdy, Mitch!" A burly, much younger version of his father with less beard and hair under a wide-brimmed black hat stepped out of the forest foliage, his rifle now held at port. "We like to not knowed you, wearing them chin whiskers. Pa and me, we was wondering who you was and why you was sneaking up us."

"Not too wise, I suppose," Mitch said. "But I didn't want to come upon you when you weren't expecting me and . . ."

"And?" Luke McGrath prompted.

"I wanted to make sure there weren't others at your place who might not want to see me."

The McGrath clan, originally from Georgia, had moved to the Ozarks as early settlers. These two back-woodsmen were typical of the Pea Ridge residents—suspicious of strangers yet generous to those they favored. Since their first meeting on the road to Texas, Luke had taken a liking to Mitch, and their friendship had ripened over time. After the war, although disapproving of outlaw activities, he and his family had sheltered both Mitch and, grudgingly, Bobby. Mitch, especially, had made friends with the small boy, Patrick.

"Been a long time, Mitch," Luke said. "You come visiting or what?"

"More like hunting," Mitch admitted. "Spent some time in state prison in Missouri for my fool outlaw days. I did my time and been minding my own business since I got out." He paused. "Then I had a run-in with an old friend."

The big man gave a derisive snort. " 'Old friend'? You mean that no-good Bob Carlin? What kind of run-in?"

By way of answer, Mitch pulled his shirttail free and lifted it to show the angry red weal on his right side.

"Gunshot?" Luke asked.

Mitch nodded. "Inch or two different, I wouldn't be here."

"Bob did that?" Pat asked, moving closer to see.

Mitch told them of the treacherous behavior of his former friend and the bank robbery, in the aftermath of which he had become an alleged participant.

Luke gave a low whistle of disbelief. "An' why was you looking for him here at *my* place?"

"We've both hidden out here at times," Mitch reminded him.

The older man shook his head emphatically. "That was then. You was one story, but that no-'count Bob Carlin warn't too welcome then, and he sure ain't welcome now. I seed him turning bad even when we left him there by Baxter Springs."

"You see him recently or know if he's here in the hills?"

"He might be," Luke mused. "I ain't seen him, but there's mebbe others around who jes' might take him in—that is, if he pays 'em whatever."

"Would you?" Mitch asked.

The big man laughed, showing a wide, white smile through his black beard. "I could use some cash money. Maybe I jes' would."

"Naw, Pa wouldn't do any such thing," Pat countered. "Time when I was a runt, Bob slapped me silly, saying how I was being a bother to him and getting underfoot."

"Nobody slaps my kin 'less'n it's me," Luke said.

"We're heading fer our noon eating," Pat said. "You want some fresh squirrel?"

"Not unless it's cooked," Mitch said with a grin.

"Come on in, then," Luke said.

Mitch retrieved his mare and, together with the two men bearing the carcasses of their morning's hunt, walked into the clearing and strode toward the log cabin. The thin woman came out onto the front porch as they approached, shading her eyes as she peered at them.

"That Mitch Ellsworth?" she called.

"It's him, sure 'nuff, Esther. Come out to see us," Luke told her.

"Land sakes," the woman said plaintively. "Ain't gonna be no trouble, is there?"

"Pleased to see you again, Mrs. McGrath," Mitch said. "I'm not bringing trouble here."

"You come, it comes," she said crossly. She turned

and reentered the cabin, slamming the screen door behind her.

"Pay her no never-mind," Luke said in a lowered voice. "I give her a hard life, so she speaks hard but don't rightly mean it."

"I wouldn't have come if I had much of choice," Mitch said apologetically. "It was just my guess that Bobby would look to hide here in these hills like he did years ago. I don't know that as a fact, but it stands to reason."

Luke nodded as they went up the two steps to the porch. "You can stay a spell 'til maybe we can find out. Sleep on the cabin floor or out in the barn?"

"Barn will do fine," Mitch responded.

"Could be he's hereabouts," Luke mused aloud again. "Whatcha fixing to do? An' whatcha need from me and my young 'un?"

"No need for either of you to get involved," Mitch cautioned.

"Well, Bob's done you a mean turn, and if we can lend a hand, we're proud to do 'er."

Mitch turned to the younger McGrath. "You've grown and filled out quite a bit since the last time I saw you."

"Big enough and got the grit to whup my Pa," Pat bragged in jest, and then he ducked to avoid the roundhouse cuff his father aimed at him.

"Old man's aim going bad too," the young man chortled as he opened the screen door and darted inside.

"Think you can still take him?" Mitch asked Luke with a laugh.

"Mebbe fer a mite more years," Luke said with a nod of conviction but with a glint of merriment in his eyes. "Then, more'n likely he'll rassle me down sooner than I'd like to think." He opened the door and waited to let Mitch walk through ahead of him.

Chapter Ten

After Esther cleared the tin plates from the table, the three men remained seated, lingering over their coffee. When she finished in the kitchen, she moved to a rocking chair near a window at the front of the cabin's main room, seated herself, and reached for a well-worn, leather-bound Bible. She opened it to a marked page and began to read silently, her lips moving.

"You still go to the crossing for Sunday meetings?" Mitch asked as he looked from her to Luke.

"Time to time," the big man answered. "Jes' a little buncha neighbors now, and we read from the Good Book." He paused. "Them that can read." He shook his head sadly. "Different when we had a preacher man coming 'round."

Mitch arched his eyebrows in question.

88

"Had a Methodist circuit-riding feller coming regular ever' now and then. Nice feller. Warn't much for preaching hell-and-damnation, but he did do a fair enough job in the marrying and the burying. He'd sprinkle them that needed to be baptized in the spirit." He gestured to the woman across the room. "Esther wanted him to say the words to make us rightly married, but he stopped coming 'round before we got to it."

The woman looked up, scowled, and then started reading again.

"Next we had us a Baptist preacher. He was kinda puke-faced and scrawny, but he was something to watch when he stood high on a stump and started shouting the devil outta us. He gone and said that the Methodist feller didn't know what in the Sam Hill he was doing. Said that nobody that only got theirselves sprinkled was ever gonna make it into heaven. Said everybody had to be dunked clear down under the water to make 'er right." He shook his head. "And that turned out bad for him."

"Something happened?" Mitch asked.

"Well, it was the wrong time of the year," Luke resumed. "We shoulda told him sooner, but that young feller waded hip deep out into the creek and was wanting folks to come out and get dunked. A couple of the young'uns started in before their kin drug 'em back when them pi-sen snakes started swarming."

"Moccasins?"

"Bit him all over 'fore we could get him out," Luke said with a sorrowful expression. "Warn't nothing we could do. He jes' laid there, shaking and carrying on." He shook his head. "We buried him and fixed him a nice pine slab for a headstone with a cross cut up there in the top of it. One of the womenfolk showed us how to spell his whole name, and we put it jes' right under that cross."

"Anybody ever come looking for him?" Mitch asked.

Luke shook his head.

"You asking about them prayer meetings. Was you fixing to go this Sunday and see if there's word about Carlin?" Luke queried.

"As I recall, after the meeting people liked to talk," Mitch said.

Luke didn't answer immediately. His brow wrinkled, and his lips pursed in thought. "Best jes' me'n Pat go and you stay put," he said finally. "If'n you go, and if Bob's hereabouts, he'll know somebody's on the hunt fer him."

"That's true enough," Mitch agreed. "But I'm putting you in the middle of this. It's not your problem."

"Glad to do 'er," Luke responded. "Maybe we was dumb ol' hillbillies to that Bob, but we was good folks according to you. 'Sides, them at the meeting ain't gonna talk with you, and, hells bells, they wouldn't take kindly having any outlander butting in on 'em."

"Luke McGrath!" the woman called. "Ain't none of your concern. We'd best stay clear of it."

"Read your Good Book," Luke reprimanded. "This here is man's business."

"If we just listen to what's being said," young Pat

said, turning his head to address both parents, "there ain't no harm in that. We hear something, we come and tell Mitch, and he can do what he wants to do about it."

"It ain't right to go to a prayer meeting for the wrong reason," his mother said harshly. "No good'll come of that."

"Ma Esther's thinking 'bout your immortal soul," Luke said. "You aiming to kill Carlin if you find him?"

Across the room, the woman gave a triumphant grunt.

"Another woman asked me that too," Mitch responded. "A woman who helped me. I got to admit, I was mad enough, and at the time I didn't know whether I would or not." He took a long breath. "Lord knows he has it coming, but, no. I'm planning on taking him alive and bringing him back to Missouri for trial."

"What about that money he stole?"

"If it's handy, I'll take it back too."

Luke gave a whoop of derision. "And I figgered that preacher was a danged fool, walking into snake water in August." He rose from the table and paced a few steps one way and then another. He stopped at the table and leaned on it, facing Mitch. "If Bob Carlin has his bunch with him, it'll be danged near the same. How you gonna pick him clean outta *them* kinda moc'sins?"

Mitch shrugged.

"Best you call this here a nice visit and head on back home," the big man advised. "Somebody, someplace, they'll do Bob, and you don't need to bother. They got you figgered dead and buried, and you ain't no need to worry no more."

"Not so," Mitch argued. "I try to go back to my place, and people will say, 'We thought you were dead.' Word gets back to Mayfield, and they go ask that woman, 'Where's that man you said you buried?' They come down hard on her and those that helped me, and where's the justice for them?" He shook his head with a keen intensity. "And, knowing I'm alive, they come after me for a robbery I wasn't a part of."

Luke resumed his seat at the table, and for a few minutes there was silence. Across the room, Esther McGrath continued to read.

Mitch broke the hush. "I bring Bob in, and, with Susan Jennings's story that I was at her place at the time the robbers were in Harrisonville, they'll likely believe me."

"You got more trust in folks than I do," Luke said. He turned to his wife. "We're going to the prayer meeting this Sunday."

"Ain't right," she snapped.

"You look in that book and see where it says about doing good and helping folks what needs it."

The woman began thumbing the pages.

"Whatcha doing, Ma?" Pat asked.

"Looking where it might say, 'Mind your own business,' " she declared.

Chapter Eleven

When Bobby came back from Texas in April of 1864, Mitch had noticed the change in him. The change made Mitch uneasy. There was impudence in his friend's bearing, a great deal of swearing and braggadocio in his talk. He had spent the winter with coarse men, and their boorishness had apparently rubbed off on him.

In the dark and still frosty spring night, Mitch and Bobby had been sitting in a group of ten men circled around one of the many campfires burning in an open area within the surrounding Missouri forest. Dozens of tents had been pitched to shelter the returned guerilla fighters.

"You don't know what the hell you missed, old pal. We had the time of our lives down there. There were pretty ladies and games of chance and . . ." Bobby made a slight attempt to lower his voice. "You should have been down there in Sherman with us *real* soldiers 'stead of shirking your duties by taking time off to hang out with your hillbilly friend there."

Mitch darted a quick glance at Luke McGrath, who was seated only a few feet away. There was no indication that Bobby's comment had been overheard.

"Yeah, since we got there, I've been hearing about your 'wartime' activities down there in Sherman," Mitch responded sarcastically. "Some pretty raunchy goings-on, I hear."

Bobby laughed. "Well, one really good thing happened. Frying-pan Sam got hisself shot and killed. Nothing more than he deserved."

"Heard some got killed who didn't deserve it," Mitch said.

With the onset of warmer weather, Mitch and Luke had left Arkansas to rejoin Quantrill's army at a secret rendezvous location in the middle of Missouri. They had been surprised when they arrived to find a considerably smaller contingent of the rebel raiders in the secluding forest. Seeking reasons for the reduced number of men, they found a couple of comrades they knew and trusted to ask. There was growing discontent about the recent defeats of the Confederacy armies and a growing sense that the South was outmanned, out-supplied, and out-fought, and the battle was soon to be lost. Men were deserting, a cause of anger and concern for their leaders.

Also, in these guarded conversations, they heard that the body of Bushwhackers that wintered in Texas had splintered into many contentious factions.

The rowdiest of them, restlessly quartered at the Mineral Springs cabin retreat, made the nearby town of Sherman their site for drunken debauchery, crude behavior, and violent rampages. Almost on a daily basis these boorish raiders shot up the town and, on occasion, attacked and even murdered citizens who were in no way sympathetic to or aligned with the Union.

William Quantrill, lax in his discipline, appeared to be losing control of this unorthodox army. Although he was regarded as a hero in a large part of the South for the raid on Lawrence, word was spreading about his participation in the atrocities committed at that town and also the wanton slaughter of helpless soldiers at the Baxter Springs massacre.

Held in contempt by most of the Confederacy's high command, supported by only a couple of generals, he was becoming even less favored by his own men. There was a growing recognition of his petty-thief history, his vainglorious nature, his voracious greed, and, worst of all, his total lack of true commitment to the causes of the Confederacy. His lack of good judgment often caused discord and rancor in the edgy troops. His trusted lieutenants began to either leave or to challenge his command. Bill Gregg, a trusted lieutenant, had departed in dismay and disgust, followed by Bill Anderson, who took sixty tough marauders with him. George Todd, his next in command, openly opposed Quantrill and was elected as the new leader of the band of guerilla soldiers.

"Is it true what they're saying about Colonel Quantrill?" Mitch asked.

Bobby nodded. "He's here with Captain George. They say they're working side by side, but the word is that Todd's calling all the shots."

"Shots to do what?"

Bobby leaned toward Mitch, his manner conspiratorial. "They're saying there's a General Price who's gonna bring more than ten thousand soldiers to take over Missouri and wipe out all the Union outfits." He paused. "Our job is to keep the Federals hopping—attack supply wagons, burn bridges, raise hell with them 'til the main body comes barreling in."

Before Mitch could respond, Luke McGrath rose and beckoned Mitch as he walked out of the firelight into the dark woods.

"What's he want?" Bobby asked.

Mitch scrambled to his feet. "Guess I'll go find out."

Behind him, Bobby arose and followed for a few steps before Luke raised a palm to halt him. "Just Mitch."

Bobby stood there for a few moments, then shrugged and walked back to seat himself again at the fire.

Luke led Mitch a short distance into the trees, still in sight of the encampment but well out of earshot of even the nearest men. He came to a stop, turned toward Mitch, and spoke in a low voice. "Me and a few more are heading out 'fore first light. You want to come along?"

"You're leaving?"

"Ain't that what I just said?"

"Why, Luke? We just now got here."

The big man, an ebony silhouette in the deep night gloom of the forest, swept his right hand toward the flickering fires of the raiders' campground. "Even from the get-go I ain't been too easy with most of them fellers. Some of them big shots was pure evil even 'fore they started, and they ain't got no better since." He paused. "We turned into murdering devils there in that Lawrence town. I ain't proud of this outfit for what they did . . . what I did. I thank the Lord I waren't one shooting them wet-behind-the-ears Yankees last fall. Heard tell they was shooting them bluebellies dead even when they was giving up."

"Bad things happen in war, Luke," Mitch countered unconvincingly.

"You do whatch *hafta* do, not 'cause you *like* doing it." Again McGrath paused. "We're cutting out 'fore dawn . . . you coming?"

Mitch didn't answer immediately. Finally, he shook his head. "No, I can't. It'd be desertion." He cleared his throat. "They'll shoot or hang you for it, Luke, if they see you going or catch up with you later."

"Hell, boy," Luke scoffed, "ain't nobody gonna catch me going. And as fer coming after me later—well, lad, you been in our home woods."

"I still think you're making a mistake."

"Your mistake is staying in this fool war," Luke told

him. "From what I'm a-hearing, the grays are getting whupped ever' time and ever' place. There's that Gettysburg and—"

"I can't and won't leave, Luke," Mitch interrupted. "I signed on 'til it ends, and, well, I still got scores to settle."

There was a long silence between them.

Then Luke extended his right hand, and Mitch took it in his. "You take care, boy. You change your mind or need a place to go . . . what I or mine can give, you know the way to find us."

"Thanks, Luke," Mitch said in a somber voice. "I won't forget what you've done for me." He blinked away tears. "Good luck to you."

"Don't go telling Bobby 'til long after we're clear," Luke warned. "Him or nobody."

"You're mistaken about Bobby," Mitch protested. "You don't know him like I do."

The big man didn't argue.

Shortly after sunup, while frying pans, coffeepots, and kettles were heating over dozens of freshly stoked fires, there was a stirring in the camp. It was not quite a commotion, but to the men preparing for breakfast, it was evident that something was out of order. Moving rapidly from group to group, a scattering of corporals, sergeants, and even officers appeared agitated in their actions. At a distance their words were unheard, but from the pantomime it was clear that each tense conversation was an interrogation.

"This have anything to do with you and Luke?" Bobby asked. The two youths were standing in a line with the others, tin plates and cups in their hands, waiting for breakfast to be served by a volunteer cook at a fire.

Mitch shook his head.

"Someone's coming at us, and he's looking straight at you," Bobby said as he nodded at a burly man with a florid face walking in a quick stride toward them. "That's Archie Lewis."

"One of you named Ellsworth?" the man, Lewis, asked loudly as he came to the line. The question was unnecessary; the man's eyes were fixed upon Mitch.

"That's me," Mitch acknowledged.

"You rode in with that big Arkansas hillbilly?" Lewis questioned.

"Been riding with Luke McGrath since last fall," Mitch said.

"Him and ten others flew the coop sometime during the night," Lewis declared, his anger further reddening his features. "That's desertion, and we've got men chasing 'em. Catch 'em, we'll string 'em up."

Mitch thought it wise not to speak.

"Did you know McGrath was deserting?" the man demanded.

"No, sir," Mitch lied. "News to me."

Lewis spoke to Bobby. "How about you?"

"Scarcely knew him," Bobby said, and he looked away.

The man squared to Mitch, his manner now threatening. "Some said you and that turncoat went out together into the woods and was talking secret last night. Tell me that wasn't so."

Before Mitch could form an answer, Bobby turned and took a half step between Mitch and his inquisitor. "There wasn't any secret talking going on. I was standing right there when the big guy went his way and Mitch went the other."

"To do what?" The question was edged with suspicion.

"To take care of nature," Bobby said with a merry smile. "What else?"

Lewis switched his hard glare back and forth between the two youths, the scowl on his face unchanged. "You better not be lying to me, sonny. We'll be keeping our eyes on both of ya. You got any thoughts 'bout deserting like that hillbilly, there'll be a noose or a bullet for each of ya."

Lewis gave a sigh of exasperation and strode away, seeking others to question.

"Saved your bacon, didn't I?" Bobby asked with a sly smile.

Mitch shrugged.

Bobby gestured to the just-opened space between Mitch and the cook waiting at the fire. "How about getting ours?"

Chapter Twelve

After the war's bitter end, the battles no longer raged, but the hostilities remained. In the Deep South, cannons were returned from the fields of combat and placed on courthouse lawns, aimed north. A great many Confederate soldiers—worn, unkempt, and unpaid, without homes or families to which to return—wandered without aim or purpose, widely regarded as traitors to the Union. Scores of vindictive victors considered them criminals and demanded harsh and ruthless punishments.

Quantrill's irregular troops, especially, were labeled as lawless murderers and not readily recognized as true members of the Confederate Army. As tales of the wartime atrocities of the Bushwhackers spread through the land, even a great number of those who had supported the southern cause came to think of them as outlaws.

Jerry S. Drake

With reputations, whether deserved or not, as desperados, Mitch and Bobby saw little reason not to ride as novice members of a newly formed bandit band led by the James brothers. The ragtag gang paused at the outskirts of a small Arkansas settlement, where, according to young Jesse, a thriving timber company kept a sizable payroll in a makeshift bank at the end of each month.

"It's not even a regular bank," Jesse crowed with smug self-assurance. "Just a storefront with an old safe in the back room. It'll be easy pickings."

Mitch didn't like the young outlaw, although Bobby seemed to idolize him. Close to Mitch's age and actually a late arrival to Quantrill's raiders, Jesse, along with his brother, Frank, had gained favor with "Bloody" Bill Anderson and Archie Clemens and ridden on several robberies with them. Young as he was, Jesse was self-important, surprisingly and scathingly intolerant of Mitch and Bobby's youth and inexperience, sarcastic, and hateful. Still, he was capable of charm and persuasion when he chose to be, then of vindictive viciousness in another facet of personality. Frank, a lanky man, older, quieter, and gruff in manner, seemed content to let his younger brother call the shots.

"You two milksops can keep watch at each end of the street while we're inside," Jesse said to the young pair. "And don'cha make a botch of it. Keep your eyes peeled for any law or gun-totin' citizens." He turned his horse and rode away.

"He's got no call to talk to us that way," Mitch complained.

"You got to learn to get along with him, Mitch," Bobby countered. "You rub him the wrong way, that's for sure."

"I don't appreciate being called a milksop," Mitch persisted.

"What's that word mean?" Hubie McGinnis asked. "It mean something bad, Mitch?"

Hubert McGinnis was the least likely outlaw either Mitch or Bobby had ever encountered. Simple in mind, easy to lead, he was a cousin of one of Quantrill's raiders and had followed his kin's involvement in the war although he had no notion of what it was all about. On the other hand, he did serve a useful function in the various outlaw bands to which he gravitated after his kinsman's death. He was a fair cook and never complained about whatever menial duties were assigned him.

"Nothing to bother your head about, Hubie," Mitch said. "Jesse's just having fun with us, I guess."

Hubie nodded, and a smile replaced his frown of worry. He, too, was entranced with the James brothers, and for good reason; both were among the few men who didn't tease or bait him. Indeed, the two seemed almost kind to him.

The gang entered the little village, riding singly or in pairs, and, as instructed, Mitch and Bobby took up surveillance positions. Jesse and Frank moseyed along the boardwalk and entered a narrow building with a hand-lettered sign that identified it both as a lawyer's office and a bank.

Mitch, feeling conspicuous at a standstill on his black gelding, was particularly uneasy, since the small town seemed quite crowded for a rural Saturday. There were many men and women moving along the boardwalks and crossing the streets, two wagons being loaded at a feed store. Three more of the gang strolled to the target building, where two of them entered while one, Hubie, remained outside.

Suddenly the muffled reports of two gunshots turned everyone's attention to the small building, and seconds later four outlaws inside rushed from the building, Frank turning to fire a shot from his handgun back through the open door. The five men ran for their horses, and from the interior of the law office a dozen husky men poured into the street, firing their rifles and revolvers after the fleeing outlaws.

A fusillade of shots rang out bullets flying everywhere. Men, women, and children on the street dashed for cover, some falling flat to the ground and hiding their heads. Horses bucked and whinnied at the uproar. A team hitched to a wagon team bolted and, driverless, dragged the careering cart toward open country.

Miraculously, the would-be robbers made it to their horses, mounted, and whipped their steeds into a frantic getaway. Mitch, stunned by the spectacle, held his horse in check, and, even as the bandits galloped past, he looked back in dismay at the unexpected carnage.

Bobby wheeled his horse toward Mitch, his eyes wide with either fright or excitement. "Come on!" he shouted. "They're after us!"

Sure enough, the pursuing men were mounting horses. To Mitch's relief, however, all the people on the street were picking themselves up, and there appeared to be no still bodies in sight.

"Come on!" Bobby shouted again, and he spurred his horse into a gallop.

Mitch turned his horse and dug his heels into its sides to follow the rest of the desperados. He looked behind and, to his dismay, saw that the angry pursuers were thundering after them and firing weapons. As bullets whistled dangerously close, he whipped the sides of his steed with the ends of the reins and bent low over its neck.

The chase continued for at least three miles on the main dirt roadway that, for a long stretch, was bordered on either side by deep, wide ditches. It would be a perilous and desperate action to veer from the country highway, to urge a horse to leap such a gap. It would likely cause, at best, a spill or, worse, a break of one of the animal's legs. The gang in flight was some distance ahead, while he and Bobby were still within gunshot range.

Far ahead, where the ditches were shallow, Mitch

saw the five riders divide, three racing to the right and into the trees, two others riding into the forest on the left. Mitch looked back over his shoulder at the closing riders and knew that he, if not Bobby, a length ahead, would be overtaken within seconds.

Mitch jerked the reins to his left and, digging his heels into the sides of his gelding and shouting a command, drove the black horse to the side of the road and, kicking again, prodded the animal into a jump.

The horse soared high, and the great, muscular effort nearly dislodged Mitch from the saddle. He hung on to the saddle horn, and as the gelding cleared the ditch, the impact nearly knocked him off again. The landing was a near thing, the back legs of the horse scrambling at the lip of the steep incline. The gelding nearly fell but then caught its footing, regained its stride, and galloped into a clearing. Mitch whipped the horse again and again, urging it toward a near by grove of trees. Behind him he heard pistol shots, but nothing came near.

He glanced back and saw the riders still on the road, their horses milling about as they aimed their weapons, but now he knew he was likely out of their range. Nonetheless, he felt relief as his gelding galloped into the cover of the woods.

He wondered and worried if Bobby had also eluded the angry mob. For ten minutes he continued riding, guiding his lathered horse at a slow walk through the trees with only a vague sense of direction.

"That was a hoot, wasn't it?" Bobby's voice came from the woods to the right.

Mitch reined his gelding to a halt and spotted Bobby sitting astride his mount in a clearing among the cottonwoods. His hat was in his hand, and he was wiping his neck with his kerchief, a wide smile on his face. "Regular hornets' nest we ran into."

"You got clear, I see," Mitch said.

"They all stopped to watch you jump," his friend responded. "They didn't think you'd make it."

"Who were those men?" Mitch asked.

"Jesse had it right about it's being payday. Trouble was, all the lumberjacks were inside, waiting to get paid." He laughed. "Guess we won't count that as much of a payday for the James gang."

"They might still be after us," Mitch cautioned. He swiveled in his saddle to scan the woodland behind him. "They likely know this territory better'n us."

"I think they quit," Bobby countered. "They scared us off, and I think they'll go back to town to brag about how they did it."

"Hope so," Mitch said. "Think everybody else got away?"

Bobby nodded. "Should've. They were ahead of us."

"They get any money?" Mitch asked.

Bobby shook his head. "I don't think so. I heard Jesse cussing up a storm—mad as hell, he was, shouting it was a bust."

"Think anybody got hurt?"

"Not that I saw."

"We going to meet up with the others?"

Again Bobby shook his head. "Jesse's got a mad on, and I sure as heck don't want to be around him." He paused. "We need a place to hole up. Word of what we just tried is going to have the law on the lookout for us."

They sat in silence for a long while.

"How about those hillbilly friends of yours?" Bobby finally asked. "Don't they live somewhere nearby?"

"I don't know about that," Mitch said uneasily. "I don't know that they'd—"

"Isn't that what friends are for?" Bobby cut in. "Let's give 'em a try."

Mitch and Bobby rode their horses into the compound of the McGrath family home. A warning shot from the house whistled over their heads, but neither young man considered himself in danger. Once close enough to be recognized, they were sure of a welcome, although most likely a reluctant one.

"Hail the house!" Bobby shouted. "It's Mitch Ellsworth and Bob Carlin!"

They reined their horses to a halt at some distance from the log structure and waited. After a long period a bear of a man stepped through the front door, his rifle held across his chest. "Boys, it ain't too smart to come galloping into my place!"

"We're here as friends!" Bobby spoke loudly. "Can we come in?"

"You come this far, I reckon a little farther ain't much more of a bother. What's this all about?" Luke McGrath asked.

The two youngsters walked their horses to a hitching rail, dismounted, and tied the reins of their animals to it. Bobby was the first to approach the big mountain man and extend his hand. "Call it a rebs' reunion."

McGrath ignored the hand. "My war's long over, even if yours ain't." He looked at Mitch. "This here your idee, young feller?"

Mitch was awkward in his stance and manner. "Sort of," he stammered. "I guess we just didn't know where else to go."

"We don't hear a lot from the outside," McGrath said, his rifle still held at the ready, "but we heard 'bout what some of ya been doing."

"Robbing people." A female voice came from inside the cabin. Esther McGrath, Luke's common-law wife, stepped out onto the porch and positioned herself a few feet to her husband's left. "I don't hold with thieving."

A young boy, the McGrath's eleven-year-old son, appeared in the doorway and gave a wide smile and a wave to Mitch.

"Law's been hard on southerners after the war," Bobby countered. "We're just trying to get by."

The woman gave a hoot of contempt.

"You're right about the robbing and stealing, Missus

McGrath," Mitch said. "We know it isn't right, and we're not going to do it anymore. We're going to get out of it."

"Why are you here?" Luke asked.

"We were wondering if we could stay for just a little while," Bobby said. "We're dead broke, and we can't go home . . . wherever that is nowadays."

"I don't hold with no night riders," Esther McGrath declared.

"We just need a place to rest up," Bobby pleaded. "Just for a couple of days?"

Luke stared at them for several moments and then turned to his wife. "I don't know about the talky one, but we know young Mitch. Couldn't hurt to give 'em a little help, could it?"

"Humph!" the woman responded. "You're the man of the house. They bring trouble; let it be on your head." With a toss of her hair, she reentered the house, grasping the hand of her boy and pulling him with her as she marched inside.

"Put your horses in the barn," Luke instructed. "Bunch up some of that straw for your sleeping, 'cause that's all we can offer." He stood there without speaking for a few moments and then added, "Come in when you're ready. Maybe the old woman will soften up and fix you somethin' to eat." He stepped close to Mitch and lowered his voice. "I done promised you help if ya ever needed it, but I'm with Ma on that outlawing. Ya need to think 'bout mending your ways." He turned and entered his house.

"That was smart, saying how we was heading down the straight and narrow," Bobby said. "They bought it, didn't they?"

"News for you, Bobby," Mitch said evenly. "I meant every word of it."

Chapter Thirteen

The yellow dog's barking roused Mitch from his memories of that long-ago day at this very same Ozark homestead. It was nearly sunset as the McGrath family came walking up the path, returning from the Sunday prayer meeting. He stretched and rose from his seat on the steps of the front porch and ambled down the walkway to meet them.

Luke, then Patrick, led the single-file procession, with Esther close behind and matching them stride for stride. The two men waved their greetings, but the woman gave him only a glacial glance and entered the back door of the cabin. The father veered toward Mitch as Pat hastened to pet the dog and quiet the animal's eager, excited behavior.

"How did it go?" Mitch asked as the older man joined him.

"Long day," Luke responded. "Didn't know us plain folks could get so all-fired wound up about sinning and saving."

Mitch waited, knowing McGrath would eventually get to the subject of his interest.

"Me and mine, we got us a ticket straight to hell, 'cause we ain't been to the meetings for a spell," Luke said. "I was gonna lay into 'em, but my old lady, she had her say first. She started naming out folks that have done a heap more worse, and that soon shut their yaps."

"Not a pleasant time?"

The big man gave Mitch a cocked-head look. "Why, no, sirree, we had us a fine, fine time. Once we finished the damn-us-to-hell business, we had us a barbecue and some fiddling and dancing 'til we was full of it all and plumb wore out."

"Do any talking?" Mitch asked. "And listening?"

Luke nodded as his son came to join them. "Seems you guessed right. I ain't got no names as such, but there's a passel of outsiders hanging 'round over at the Jessup place."

"Carlin and his bunch?" Mitch asked.

Luke shrugged. "Can't tell for sure, but I'd say so."

"Do I know the Jessups?"

"Naw," Luke said. "We never would have had ya dealing with the likes of them—had no use for Amos

Jessup and his bunch." He paused. "Back in them years I recall you was gone elsewhere when young Bobby got nasty with my missus and my boy. I kicked his tail outta here, and I heard he paid the Jessups to take him in." Again he paused. "Likely he might be there now."

"Betcha that's where," Pat said. "I'll just betcha."

"How far to their place?" Mitch asked.

"A fair walk," Luke said. "We'll take it at twilight."

"Tonight?" Mitch asked.

"That's what you come for, ain't it?"

"No need for you to get involved," Mitch said. "Just set me a course."

Luke shook his bushy head. "You don't know these woods."

Mitch started to object, but Luke raised a warning hand.

"All right, then," Mitch agreed. "Your call."

"Mind ya," Luke cautioned, "this here is a look-see, no shooting or trying to make a grab."

Mitch nodded. "Lay of the land—I understand."

"Let's see what my old lady is fixing for supper," Luke said with a tilt of his head toward the cabin. "She's beginning to recollect how she likes ya—she's fixing to pan-fry some venison and sliced potatoes."

"She likes me?"

Mitch marveled at the ease and pace of the two Mc-Graths as they led him in the evening gloom of the dense woods. In addition to the difficulties of stepping along the ground in the dark, he was hard-pressed to keep up with them, still weakened by his gunshot injury. He was equally awed at the silence of their advance, his own occasional missteps and the resultant noises bringing quick, reproving turns of their silhouetted heads.

After a long and heavy-breathing trek, Luke came to sudden, crouching halt, his hand raised to warn Pat and Mitch. Barely discernible in the dim light, he motioned for Mitch to come to him, his left forefinger touching his lips for absolute quiet. Mitch looked carefully where he stepped, making sure to break no twig under his tread, to rustle no leaves with his presence.

"Jessup's place is just ahead," Luke whispered. "We'll move a mite closer and lay in the weeds and see what they's about."

The trio moved a dozen feet farther and hid themselves in a stand of undergrowth at the edge of an open tract. Mitch knelt and parted the bushes to survey the scene before them. Seen in the fading light of dusk, the dwelling in the middle of the grassland swath was similar to the McGrath compound's building, but the log cabin, with oil lamps shining in two windows, was larger. Several horses stood in the corral, and there was lamplight and human movement in the barn. After a few minutes two men came out of the barn, walked across the backyard, and entered the rear of the cabin.

"Could you make 'em out?" Luke whispered.

"A little too dark," Mitch replied softly. "I don't think either one was Carlin. I'd know him."

Mitch and the McGrath men maintained their surveillance for another hour and were rewarded by the occasional appearances of the cabin's occupants. They observed several men, two women, and two small children, a boy and a girl, at various outdoor activities.

"That one," Mitch whispered finally, nodding at a man lighting his pipe on the front porch, the flame giving fleeting illumination to his features. "Hard to see from this distance, but I'm pretty sure he was one of those with Bob."

"You don't see Bob?" Pat questioned.

Mitch shook his head. "If he's there, he's staying inside."

"I can't get a good count on 'em, but there's a bunch," Luke whispered. "And that don't count Amos and his two boys."

"How will they side?"

"You go in on your own ag'in the bunch, they'll likely side with Bob."

Mitch nodded. "Getting him alone is going to be a puzzler."

There was a long period in which no one spoke.

"We seen all we're gonna see," the older man said. "Let's git."

Moving carefully and quietly, the three men retreated, leaving the Jessup farmstead behind. A few minutes later, well out of earshot, they resumed conversation in normal but low tones.

"What about the women and the kids?" Mitch asked.

"Well, there's the old lady who belongs to Amos," Luke told him. "Then there's one of their sons and his missus. Them young tads is his and hers."

"I don't want them to get hurt," Mitch said. "I'm hoping to catch Bob when he's alone."

"Maybe we can help," Pat murmured. "Maybe draw them others out some way."

"Hell, no." Mitch's voice was harsh in intensity if not in volume. "It's not your fight."

"We owe ya," Luke said.

Mitch knew what lay behind the comment. "I did nothing more than what anyone would have done."

"Taking on a cougar bare-handed?" Luke reminded him. "When it was chawing on young Pat there?"

Mitch well remembered the incident. He and Bob had taken the young boy to a stream for afternoon fishing during their stay those many years ago. With lines in the water, neither had noticed the youngster wander away from the creek. It was the scream of the mountain lion that had galvanized Mitch into action. He had leaped to his feet and raced into the surrounding woods just in time to see the fearsome animal attack the fleeing child. Mitch had yelled at the top of his lungs and charged the animal.

"My being bigger just scared him off," Mitch said softly.

Pat grinned and pointed to his left buttock. "Chunk of

meat he took off with puckered up that cheek there." He chuckled. "I recollect how Mitch hauled off and socked that old puma to kingdom come. Danged cat was so spooked, it run off back into the trees."

"My young'un in the woods without no gun or hunting knife was a danged fool," Luke said. "And so was a growed man who shoulda knowed better than to fistfight a mountain lion." He paused. "But that's the kinda fool I'm grateful to."

"Bob had his gun," Pat said. "You'da figgered he'd come a-running 'stead of Mitch, but he didn't show up 'til it was all over."

Luke grunted.

"That still is no reason for you all to get involved now," Mitch protested.

"Our choice—ain't yours," the older man growled.

They trudged on for several moments.

"Your wife had it right," Mitch said.

In the darkness, Luke's head turned.

"I've brought you trouble."

Esther McGrath closed her Bible as the three men entered the cabin. "You need something to eat?"

Luke looked at the others and then shook his shaggy head. "You can git on to bed if that's your aim. We got some talking to do, and I'll be in when we git 'er done."

"Don't go and make no mess in the kitchen," she warned as she strode to the doorway of their bedroom. "I ain't cleaning it up at daybreak if you do."

She entered the bedroom and closed the door behind her as Mitch and the McGrath men seated themselves at the table. For a short while no one spoke.

"You got something figgered?" Luke asked.

"I'm working on it."

"You gotta cut him outta the herd," Luke said, tenting the fingers of his hands on the tabletop. "Anything we can do to make that happen?"

"There's two times when he never abides having company."

A sly smile appeared on Pat's face.

Mitch chuckled. "Unless he's changed his ways, fishing on his lonesome was what *I* had in mind."

Chapter Fourteen

Four days later, Mitch sat again in the tall brush over-looking the Jessup farmhouse with a borrowed .44 caliber rifle. It was his third day of watching, waiting patiently for a sight of his quarry. Thanks to the loan of a spyglass from Luke, he was able to peer closely at the occupants of the house. He was mindful of any flashes of the sun reflecting off the lens and kept it shaded at all times. On the second day of his surveillance, Bob Carlin appeared twice briefly—on the front porch of the cabin late in the afternoon and at the corral around dusk. Mitch kept his vigil for ten to twelve hours each day, hoping to see Carlin separate from the rest.

Maybe he gave up fishing, Mitch considered.

Today, with the sun slanted at a midafternoon angle,

120

Bob came out of the back door of the cabin, fishing gear in hand. Mitch's initial elation gave way to disappointment as two of the outlaw gang, similarly equipped, followed Carlin as he headed into the woods behind the Jessup compound.

"Mebbe your best chance to get 'im," a hushed voice said from the underbrush behind him.

Mitch turned to see Luke step out of the forest foliage with a Sharps rifle in his hands, a canvas pack on his back.

"For a big man, you sure do creep up on a fellow," Mitch whispered as McGrath came close and knelt beside him.

"Huntin' puts meat on the table," the big man responded. "Them two there's gonna be a problem."

"Maybe not," Mitch said softly. "If I know Bob, he'll move away from them. He won't fish with them."

"Well, that's a comfort, I 'spose. Pick up your gear, and let's go. We don't need to follow. I reckon I can make out 'bout where they's headed."

Twenty minutes later they took cover behind a thick cluster of forest shrubs, looking down a steep embankment. The three outlaws had stopped at a bend of a rushing stream where the water had eddied into a lazy, swirling pool. The two henchmen were obviously planning to fish at this location, baiting their hooks. Carlin, for a moment involved in conversation, turned and walked along the bank, heading upstream.

"Won't catch much, if any," McGrath whispered. "Water runs too fast." He scowled, his bewhiskered face fearsome. "We ain't no option 'cept takin' 'em at gun-point." He paused. "You got that?"

Mitch nodded. "I'll go after Bob—"

"Nope, I can take 'im better'n you." The big man's soft voice was emphatic. "You ain't got the sneaking-up skills, and, 'sides, Bob's gonna figger that you ain't gonna pull no trigger on him. And he'd likely figger that right."

Mitch started to argue, then gave a rueful smile.

"Bob knows I'd kill him if I had to," Luke said with grim intensity. "I'll try to take him quiet-like, but if you hear shooting, it might be him or it might be me. No matter which, you hear it, you kill them two down there and hightail it outta here as fast as you can go."

"Be careful with Bob," Mitch warned. "Taking him won't be easy."

McGrath nodded. "I'll coldcock 'im if'n I can get close 'fore he sees me." He reached to touch his back-pack. "If I do 'er right, I got stuff to hogtie and plug his mouth so's he can't make no hollerin'." He bobbed his head to indicate the outlaws now with lines in the pool. "I know ya ain't a mind to do 'er, but I'd put them two away whether we get Bob or not. That'd be two less to worry about."

"Shots would likely bring the others."

McGrath's toothy smile showed through the whiskers. "Not if you do it right. Walk right up to 'em while they's fooling with their fish poles and gut-shoot 'em with your pistol. Poke the barrel into their belly fat, and it ain't gonna make 'nuff noise to carry."

"I'm glad I wasn't one of those Lincoln boys you met during the war," Mitch said with a sigh.

Again the big man smiled. "Nothin' ag'in 'em. They did what they saw as their duty, and I did mine." He glanced up at the sunlight filtering through the leafy canopy. "I 'spect he's far enough away now."

Suddenly Luke was gone.

If anyone can take Bob by surprise, it'll be McGrath, Mitch mused. For all of his height, girth, and mass, the big man moved through the forest with stealth equal to that of any other predatory woodland creature. Mitch concentrated his sight and attention on the two men sitting on the bank sixty feet away. He recognized one of them as the fellow Bob had called Nate, the belligerent outlaw who had seemed intent on confrontation. He remembered the other only vaguely, one of those at a distance during his rendezvous with Bob.

The two outlaws, with their raucous laughter and frolicsome behaviors, were easy targets. Mitch trained his rifle on the narrow-faced ruffian who had been spoiling for a fight at their first encounter. His finger touched the trigger, the thought crossing his mind that any innocents who chanced into a disagreement or conflict with this venomous man would likely die. Those unknown and future victims would surely be saved if he now pressed that trigger. He grimaced and shook such thoughts from his mind.

After a short while McGrath returned and motioned for Mitch to rise and follow him. With a last look at the men below, Mitch crept away from his vantage site, trying his best to walk softly. After moving a considerable distance away from the stream, McGrath stopped to speak aloud. "He's gone."

Mitch blinked his lack of understanding.

"Gone," McGrath repeated. "Found his gear on the ground and horse droppings where he'd tied his mount. Likely snuck the horse out early 'fore anyone noticed." He paused. "Looks like he lit out on them others."

It took a few seconds for Mitch to collect his thoughts, and finally he gave a rueful smile. "Took off with all the money, I suspect."

"Them others are gonna be mad if that's what he's gone and done," his friend said.

"Any signs of which way he headed?" Mitch asked as the two men started walking.

"Tracks lead into them woods. He'll likely circle wide 'round the house and try to get to that wagon road 'fore anybody misses him."

"I need to get to my horse and go after him," Mitch said as he and Luke weaved their way through the trees. "He's got a head start, but maybe I can catch up."

"Any idee which way he'll go?"

"He won't head back into Missouri," Mitch said. "Likely heading southwest."

Luke cocked his head in a questioning way.

"Lots of territory to get lost in, and less law trying to cover it all," Mitch ventured.

"Gut feeling?" Luke said.

Mitch nodded. "That and something he said about sitting under some palm trees. I figure that's Texas, Mexico, or maybe even out in the south part of California."

"Good a guess as any," the big man said, and he lengthened his stride and motioned for Mitch to hurry behind him.

Mitch swung up onto his horse and reached down to grasp Luke's hand. "Thanks for your help. We did give it a try."

"Close but no ringer," Luke agreed. "Want Pat and me to go with ya?"

Mitch shook his head. "Appreciate the offer, but you've done enough already. You helped me find Bob, and now it's up to me."

"Even if you take him, how're you going to drag him by your lonesome all the way back up north?" Luke persisted.

"*If* I find him, I'll work it out," Mitch replied. "I'm not even sure I'll be tracking him in the right direction."

"If ya do find him, you'd best kill him," Luke said. "He'll do it to you 'fore you get him home."

"I'll be extra careful," Mitch assured him. "I'll get word to you how it goes."

"We'd like to know," the younger McGrath said in

earnest. "Want us to put some hurt on them that Bob left behind?"

Mitch gave him a grin in return. "Let them be. They'll be running here and there when they find out what he's done to them. They're a sorry bunch, and they'll saddle up and be on their way before nightfall. Let them ride on out, and good riddance."

To his surprise, Esther McGrath came out the door of the cabin with a small cloth bag in her left hand. She descended the steps and walked to join her menfolk.

"Mrs. McGrath," Mitch said, "I surely—"

"You'll be needing some eating as you go," she cut in, the tone of her voice brusque. "Ain't much but some turnips, carrots, and 'taters from my garden, but they'll have to do ya." She raised the sack, offering it to him.

Mitch took the bag with one hand and touched the brim of his hat with the other. "They surely will, ma'am. I thank you."

"Don't go taking no chances with that evil man," she said, the curt tenor of her speech softening. "I ain't quite made up my mind about you, but I surely have about that no-good Robert Carlin."

"I'll be careful, I promise," Mitch responded. "And someday I hope you'll see me in a better light."

"Go on with you now," she said. She turned and marched back toward the cabin, never looking back as she disappeared inside.

"Yep, she likes ya," Luke said. "Wouldn't give stuff outta her garden if she didn't."

"As she said, I'd best go on," Mitch said. "He may have four, five hours ahead of me, maybe twice that much." With a wave of his hand, he pressed Belle into a trot.

"Good luck to ya!" Luke called. "Don't getcha self kilt!"

Chapter Fifteen

Leaving Arkansas, Mitch had followed the likely direction he believed Bob Carlin would take to a southwestern destination. Moving through the Oklahoma Territory toward Texas involved a journey across the Indian Nations. Mitch had ridden back roads to the old southern passageway of the Butterfield Stagecoach route that coursed down from Missouri to Fort Smith and then through the Territory and on to Sherman and El Paso in Texas.

Deep now into the Chickasaw Indian sector, with evening storm clouds billowing in the west, thunder rumbling, and lightning streaking, Mitch was cheered to see one of the original way station facilities straight ahead.

John Butterfield had won a mail contract for his proposed overland stage line and, beginning in 1857, launched an enterprise that included building such stage stations every twenty miles along the lengthy southern route to the west coast. Each facility supplied fresh horses and mules for harness replacements and employed agents, blacksmiths, and helpers as well as, in appropriate stations, cooks to provide meals for passengers.

Butterfield's expensive operation lasted only until 1861. With stage lines on northern routes competing with shorter time-and-distance journeys and then, especially, with the intensified construction of new railroads, the mail contract was cancelled. After the Butterfield line sold out, various stagecoaches still traveled segments of the road, but to a much lesser degree.

Mitch rode into the station yard, dismounted, and entered the long, adobe-brick facility. Compared to most, this one was relatively neat and clean. The rectangular main room at the front of the building featured a large, multipaned window in the front wall, a sitting area with a soot-blackened fireplace at one end, and a dining area at the other. A long, heavy plank table and eight cane chairs occupied that space for stage passengers' meals. Adjacent to the dining area he could see a small kitchen with a door to the outside and, nearby, a passageway that likely led to living quarters at the back of the building for the station agent. A third door, visible at the far end of that hallway, provided a shorter route to the stable and outbuildings at the rear of the facility.

In a corner, a burly older man with a white-wreathed bald head and a salt-and-pepper bushy beard sat at an opened rolltop desk in earnest conversation with a weather-wizened Indian man sitting in a cane-backed chair beside him. Both men looked up as Mitch walked to the center of the room.

"I'm Ed Gilchrist, station agent," the burly man said as he rose from his chair and nodded to his Indian companion. "This is Joseph, my friend and helper."

"Pleased to meet you," Mitch said.

Joseph gave a little bob of his head in acknowledgment, smiled, and walked from the room.

"Mr. Gilchrist, I—"

"Just call me Ed—no *mister,* if you please."

"Wallace Ellsworth . . . Ed." Mitch introduced himself, using his detested first name. "Just rode in," he explained. "Storm coming."

The agent walked toward Mitch, his hand outstretched. "Heard the thunder. You're welcome to stay dry. Your horse outside?"

Mitch nodded and shook the man's hand.

"Put it in the shed with the rest of the stock. We got room," Gilchrist told him.

Mitch hesitated. "I'm okay. How much for sheltering my horse?"

"Aw, no need for that," the man said, showing a wide smile. "I ain't much of a person to put a man and his animal out in the weather." He gave Mitch an appraising look. "You from around here or traveling through?"

"Saddle tramp, you might call me," Mitch said ruefully. "I'm heading for Texas."

"Well, long as you ain't ashamed to admit it," Gilchrist said without losing his smile. "Can't offer you a place to bunk, but you can stay out of the wet and sleep in the barn if you want."

"I'd appreciate that." Mitch paused and then asked, "I was supposed to meet up with a fellow, head of red hair, 'bout my same size and age. We were supposed to meet and travel together, but I got delayed a couple of days, and he likely moved on without me." Again he paused. "Anybody who fits that description come through lately?"

Gilchrist nodded, his smile fading a bit. "Matter of fact, sounds like a man came through here yesterday, saying he was heading down to Sherman. Friend of yours, you say?"

"Just someone to ride with on the trail."

"He ain't far ahead, but maybe you'd be best off traveling on your own."

Mitch cocked his head, a question in his eyes.

"Wasn't nothing really, but I didn't like your friend much," the station agent said with a dismissive shrug. "He stopped in here, kinda acted like a big shot. He cussed at a couple of my Indians just 'cause they was such."

Mitch gave a slow, acknowledging nod. "He can rub folks the wrong way," he said, then enhanced his story. "I wouldn't call him a friend, but, still, it makes better sense to travel rough country together with him rather than going alone."

Gilchrist shrugged the topic away and then asked, "You got a need for some supper?"

"I've got some food in my saddlebags," Mitch told him.

"Had my evening meal already," the agent said. "But I got leftovers I could fix up."

"I've got my own—"

"Nonsense," Gilchrist interrupted, and he waved Mitch toward the table. "Take care of your horse, then come back and sit yourself down while I heat up some of them vittles. Hot meal on a rainy night ought to do your insides some good."

As if to punctuate his words, lightning flashed close by, followed by a tremendous thunderclap.

"That was close," Mitch observed. "I'd better go see if Belle is still standing."

He took the nervous mare to the large shed next to the barn, took off the saddle, and did a quick job of brushing her down before stabling her with more than a dozen of the station's team horses. With his saddlebags and the gunnysack in hand, he hurried through the strong wind that was sweeping ahead of the storm. He entered the agency building just as the first sheet of rain peppered his back and drummed on the door he slammed behind him.

"Blew in just in the nick of time," the agent said, now sitting alone at the table in the room. "Gonna have a dad-burned frog-strangler 'fore morning." He gestured to a plate of food. "Have at it."

Mitch nodded his thanks and sank onto a chair across

from Gilchrist. He picked up a fork and knife and began to saw the warmed-over beefsteak on a tin plate. The meat was tough, a little hard to chew, but warm and full of flavor nonetheless. With hot coffee to wash it down, Mitch ate slowly, savoring each bite.

The wind-driven rain was continuing to gust against the structure, and tendrils of water snaked under the front door. Gilchrist rummaged through a supply closet, found a bundle of gunnysacks, selected two, and wedged them at the base of the door to dam the flow.

"Happens every storm," the agent said as he returned to join Mitch at the table. "Floor slants in. Been meaning to fix it ever since I been here."

"You want my help fixing it in the morning?" Mitch asked with a grin.

Gilchrist returned the smile. "No call to do 'er when she's dry."

Mitch finished his meal and pushed the plate away, then reached for the coffee. "Stage business holding steady?"

The agent shrugged. "So-so. Expecting the westbound tomorrow 'bout noon." He paused. "I started with the Butterfield outfit back when I was a lot younger. Nowadays the stage comes through a couple times a week, still carrying mail-order stuff and local passengers. The short runs hold up okay. Folks nowadays'd rather take the danged trains if they's going far."

"Can't blame them. Bumping and bouncing all the way to California wouldn't be much fun."

"Well, on the other hand, I'd say it ain't much fun breathing in all that engine smoke in them summertime cars with all them windows open, I betcha."

"Well, at least they get there a lot faster," Mitch countered. "Still, the stagecoach surely has opened up the country. We ought to be mindful and thankful of that."

They lingered for some time at the table, the agent obviously eager to have a conversation with someone from the outer world.

"My Chickasaws give me some company, and they do what work I can't do for myself, but I don't get a lot of time with 'em for palaver. They got their ways that're mysterious to me, and mine don't make a lot of sense to them." He shook his head and smiled. "I don't know if they like me or just put up with me."

"Maybe some of both," Mitch said, returning the smile.

Gilchrist rose and stretched. "I'm going to head on to bed. If the rain don't let up, you can sleep as best you can over in one of them easy chairs."

"If the storm breaks a little, I'll head for the barn, where I can lie down."

"Suit yourself," the agent said with a yawn. "See you in the morning, 'less you figgering on a crack-o-dawn start."

"Depends," Mitch said as he rose from his chair and picked up his plate.

"I'll take that," Gilchrist said. "Got an Indian woman comes in early. She'll do the wash-up and cook some bacon and fried mush."

Mitch handed him the plate, finished the last of the coffee in his cup, and handed that to him as well.

"Good night, young feller."

"Good night to you," Mitch responded. "Thank you for a kind heart."

"Land sakes, I've run low on cash more 'n once in my life," Gilchrist told him. "You do someone else a favor some one of these days, and that'll make 'er even." The agent entered the passageway and padded down the hall.

Mitch walked across the main room and paused at the front window to look out at the storm. Rain was falling steadily, a heavy downpour that would turn the station grounds, corral, and roads into mire by morning. Even if the sun came out bright, clear, and hot, it would be nigh on ten o'clock before the muck dried out.

He turned from the window and seated himself in one of the cushioned chairs. It was gratifying to know that Bob was not far ahead of him. With luck, the storm had driven his quarry into shelter as it had him. A wish, deliciously malicious to be sure, crossed his mind that Bob might be out in the open in this drenching storm, soaked to the skin and miserable.

No matter the distance, Mitch knew he would eventually catch up. He would push Belle as much as he dared, though not so hard as to cause harm to the horse. When he closed the distance, his advantage would be that Bob would think him dead.

A disadvantage: Bob would be on guard against the

possible pursuit of an angry gang of cutthroats cheated out of their bank-robbery loot.

Mitch rested his head against the cushion of the chair and considered other possible dangers. There were no assurances that he, alone, would know the likely path Carlin would take to the southwest. Those hard men he had seen at the grove might be on the road behind him, riding hard to catch their treacherous leader and the money he carried. If they came this way, the gang might pass him by or, Mitch thought bleakly, recognize him. He stroked the beard on his face and was thankful for the considerable growth.

With the rain drumming on the roof and the thunder muttering, Mitch felt his eyelids growing heavy. He struggled for a few minutes to stay awake, listening for the storm to lessen in intensity. As a penniless traveler, it would be fitting for him to sleep in the barn, he considered, but the argumentative dialogue in his mind was never completed.

He slept.

Chapter Sixteen

Many years ago, it was midnight when Mitch rapped softly on the Lebanon bungalow door. In all the years since his departure with Bobby to join Quantrill's raiders, this was only his second visit home. His parents' fortunes had not been greatly enhanced but had taken a turn for the better. Through hard work and perseverance, his father's part-time work at the lumberyard had escalated into a manager's position, and his mother had taken a position teaching several grades in an outlying one-room schoolhouse. Mitch's sister, Emma, at age eighteen, had married the son of a well-to-do family, and a portion of their rich Missouri farmland had been deeded to the young couple.

The door opened only a few inches, and Jacob Ellsworth, in his nightshirt, peered out cautiously. "Mitchell?"

"Yeah, Pa," Mitch whispered. "May I come in?"

There were several seconds of hesitation, and then the door opened wider.

"I won't come in if you don't want me," Mitch said, an edge of resentment in his voice.

"Come on in," his father said brusquely.

"Who is it, Jacob?" His mother's voice came from the back of the house. "Is it Mitch?"

Mitch stepped inside, his father closing the door quickly behind him. The two men regarded each other in silence, neither making an effort to close the gap between them. His father, in fact, half turned away.

His mother, older and grayer, came out of their bedroom, tying her robe around her, and, upon seeing her son, hurried toward him. "Mitch, Mitch," she murmured wistfully. "Son, you've come home."

"Ma," he said softly, and he gathered her to him, hugging her close. "I surely wish I could've come more often."

"They after you, son?" Jacob asked, his voice ragged and demanding.

"Some are, I guess," Mitch said, still embracing his mother. "I don't think anybody knows I'm in the area."

"Jacob," Jennifer said, breaking away to face her husband. "He's home, and don't you fuss at him."

" 'Fuss?' " Jacob questioned. "He's far past 'fussing' at. I ought to swing my foot at his bottom—that's more like it."

Mitch's mother took three steps to her husband, pulling

her son toward Jacob. "Whatever he's done, whatever he is," she admonished, "he's ours—yours and mine."

Close now, father, son, and mother stood as a human triangle, Mitch and Jacob face-to-face. Slowly the anger in his father's face slipped away, and he reached out both arms to gather his wife and son to his chest.

"Pa, I'm done with outlawing," Mitch said in a low voice. "I've come home to see you, but that's not the only reason."

"What's the other reason?" his mom asked with anxiety in her voice.

"I'm going to turn myself in," Mitch told them. "I'm going to do that before they come and get me."

There was a long silence, regret in his father's expression, dismay in mom's.

"Did you kill anybody when you were riding with the outlaw gangs?" his father asked solemnly.

"No, sir," Mitch answered. "Worst thing we did—"

" 'We'? Who do you mean . . . 'we'?" Jacob interrupted.

"Bob Carlin and me," Mitch answered. "Worst thing we ever really did was to steal, and we didn't steal very much."

"Anybody get killed by the other men?" his father persisted.

"Maybe at other times, but not while we were with them," Mitch responded.

"Can you prove that?"

Mitch shook his head. "When I go to the law, I'll tell

them where and when I was in on the robberies. If they check, they'll find out that no one was shot or killed."

"They'll likely not believe you're telling the whole truth," his father said. "It may go hard with you."

"Jacob." His mother spoke, a flutter of panic in her speech. "Maybe he shouldn't—"

"No, he's right in what he's doing," Jacob cut in gently. "It's better this way, Jenn. Staying on the run, he'll likely be shot on sight when they come for him." He paused. "I'll walk him to the sheriff's office in the morning."

Mitch shook his head. "I can't let you do that," he argued. "I 'spect it's been bad enough having to face people in town for what I've done, for me being a criminal and—"

"It hasn't been that bad," his mother interrupted. "Some people say things, but most are good and seem to understand. A lot of young men fought in the war, and—"

"Not with Quantrill, Bloody Bill, and those who wouldn't quit after Lee gave it up," Mitch interjected.

"I'll walk him to the sheriff's office in the morning," Jacob repeated. "And I'll stand against any man who makes anything of it."

"Enough," Jennifer said, and she pulled her son back into her arms. "We'll rest 'til after sunrise, have a good breakfast, and, for what little time we have, it'll be almost like it used to be."

At seven o'clock the following morning, Mitch gave his tearful mother a hug and kiss, then stepped out into the bright sunlight to join his father on the front walk. Jacob Ellsworth opened the picket-fence gate, and they moved out onto the flagstone path to start the three-block walk to the business center of the town.

Women were already at work in their yards, and a couple of old men were puttering in theirs, and, as father and son passed by, most looked up with friendly smiles that quickly faded into questioning expressions at the sight of Mitch.

"Be truthful, Pa," Mitch said as they walked. "How badly have I hurt the family?"

"Like your mother said, not so bad."

"Are you being truthful?"

His father shrugged. "Wasn't much of a problem while you were fighting the war. By the time you got into the other, we'd already made a lot of friends, been regular and active at our church, gotten to know people in our work. Most folks were okay."

"But after I turned outlaw?"

His father didn't answer right away. They walked the length of a second block before he did. "Maybe a dozen and then maybe a half dozen more have made comments. A couple of hotheads tried to get me fired from my job, and some tried the same for your mom. Didn't think she should be teaching school, saying that she hadn't taught *you* right." He shook his head. "The talk wasn't taken to heart by anyone who really counted, and it didn't do us much harm. It's mostly old hat now."

"But it's still there, isn't it?"

Jacob nodded slowly. "No getting around that, I guess. We'll live with it, and so it has to be with others." They continued walking briskly, came to a corner at the town center, and started down the boardwalk. Jacob spoke again. "You were too young to go to war, and you did some fool things, but what you're doing now . . . well, it takes a lot of grit to volunteer to pay the price. I 'spect people will respect that and put your mistakes out of their minds."

"I'm sorry," Mitch said. "Sorrier than I can ever say."

"Like I said, you're doing the right thing.

"What about Emma?" Mitch asked. "How'd folks treat her?"

Jacob gave a smile. "She gave as good as she got. Didn't hurt that she was prettier than most in town."

"I'll bet it was the ugly young ladies who made most of the catcalls," Mitch said, returning the grin.

"Emma did all right for herself," Jacob acknowledged. "She put the scorn to many young bucks who tried to call on her, and she beat out every young miss by marrying up with the catch of the town." He nodded to confirm his opinion. "You'll have to meet your brother-in-law." He chuckled. "Good family, strong, sturdy man with a good head on his shoulders. She did fine."

As they walked past a mercantile store, a tall man near Jacob's age walked out, a wide smile coming to his face as he stepped up to intercept the pair. "Good morning to you, Jacob," he said in warm and cheerful greeting.

"Morning to you, Ray." Jacob returned the greeting as he and Mitch stopped walking.

After Jacob shook the man's hand, Ray turned his attention to Mitch. "And who might this young fellow be?"

Neither Ellsworth responded right away.

"It isn't . . ." The tall man's voice trailed off.

"Ray Allison," Jacob said, turning to place his hand on Mitch's left arm, "this is my son, Mitchell Ellsworth . . . my dearest son, of whom I'm very, very proud."

Without another word Jacob touched the brim of his hat in farewell and resumed his walk with Mitch, both men resolute in their purpose and their stride.

Chapter Seventeen

Morning came brightly, with sunlight streaming through the station window, flooding the room. Mitch awoke with a grimace of distress at the stiffness he felt from sleeping in a chair. He yawned and rose quickly, stretching to limber his sinews and ligaments.

"Good morning to you!"

Mitch turned to see Ed Gilchrist standing in the hallway from the back of the station house, a steaming mug of coffee in his hand.

"Morning," Mitch responded, and he made a sheepish gesture toward the upholstered chair. "Never made it to the barn."

"Makes no never-mind," Gilchrist said, and he walked to the front door. He opened it and stood in the sunshine, shading his eyes. Rain-fresh air swept in and brought

144

welcome relief from the room's stale atmosphere. "Great morning," the agent declared, nodding in agreement with his own cheerful judgment. "I was hoping you hadn't moved on yet." He turned away from the door. "That Chickasaw woman will be here any minute now to fix me a meal. Ain't no chore for her to fix enough for two."

"That rain muddied up any thoughts I had for an early ride," Mitch admitted. "About that breakfast though, it's not right for me to keep on taking handouts."

"Seems to me we covered that last night. Ain't no reason to chaw it over again." Gilchrist jerked a thumb toward the corridor. "Find yourself a cup of coffee, and we'll wait 'til the old woman comes."

Mitch strolled into the kitchen, poured coffee into a mug, and rejoined the agent at the table. "You say the stage will be through about noon?"

"More like late afternoon, if the roads dry out good enough to wheel on," Gilchrist ventured. "You want to hole up here for a day or two? I could use your help. You could earn some traveling money if you want. Maybe two or three dollars."

"Place to sleep last night was pay enough," Mitch said, mindful of Bob Carlin's lead. "What kind of help you need?"

"Changing the six-up with fresh horses after the stage comes in."

"You don't get help from folks 'round here?"

The agent screwed his face into a comical expression. "Why, sure, my Chickasaws are doing okay. You 'member that ol' Indian feller I was talking to when you showed last evening?"

Mitch nodded.

"Well, Joseph, he's my regular, but he was a-telling me he had someplace he just had to go and wouldn't be around today." He paused. "He'll be back tomorrow, but it might leave me handling all the chores 'til he does."

Mitch gave it some thought, worried that Bob might get too far ahead. "I guess that's the least I should do."

"This feller you're looking for," Gilchrist said, the usual cheer in his features now turned sober. "I got to thinking 'fore I fell asleep. I'm thinking you ain't just joining up with him . . . like maybe you're chasing after him. Reckon I got that right?"

Mitch didn't respond.

"I figger that you ain't the law—I can tell that—so what's he done to ya?"

Mitch shook his head. "Not too many questions, my friend. You've already asked more than I can answer." He paused. "Or that I care to."

Gilchrist sat quietly for a few seconds and then nodded. "All right, then, that ain't none of my business, but you seem a nice young buster, and I didn't care for that other feller, not at all. No need to take my advice, but I think he'll be a heap of trouble if you ride after him."

"There's more trouble if I don't," Mitch said, more to himself than in answer.

The noise of a door opening at the side of the building

diverted their attention, and Gilchrist rose slowly from the table. "There's the cook," he said. "Best I get her going."

The stagecoach arrived near one-thirty in the afternoon. The station agent and Mitch walked out to wave and shout their greetings to the driver and another man, the conductor, who rode on the high seat next to him.

"I warn't figgering on you 'til later!" Gilchrist shouted. He looked at the mud-splattered coach. "Been through some muck, I see."

"Just the last couple of miles 'fore we got here," the driver said as he dropped to the ground. He took off his heavy leather gloves and, using them, started flicking the dust from his clothing. "Your big storm hit mostly west of us last night and then let up. We run good and dry most of this morning."

"It weren't *my* storm, but she were a danged good 'un 'round here, you betcha." Gilchrist chuckled. "Max Sutton, meet Mr. Wally Ellsworth." The agent introduced the driver and then turned to the man moving around the lead team and approaching. "This is his topside partner, Ben Cooley."

Mitch shook hands with both hefty men as Gilchrist helped the passengers step out to stretch their legs. Three men and a young woman with a small boy gave grudging thanks and proceeded to grumble about the hard, sweltering ride.

"Got food on the table inside," Gilchrist announced.

"Nothing fancy, but it'll fill you up nice and proper." He paused. "The outhouse is 'round back if you need." Ignoring their muttered complaints, Gilchrist led them into the station to the cold lunch that awaited them.

The driver, Sutton, paused to speak to Mitch. "You working here?"

Mitch shook his head. "Just helping out for the day. Ed's regulars are off somewhere."

Sutton nodded and sauntered toward the station building, Cooley falling into step beside him.

Two minutes later Gilchrist hurried back and, with Mitch's help, unhitched the horses from the coach and led them into the corral. Then, each leading a fresh horse from the shed, they hitched the first animals into the rigging and repeated the chore, pair by pair, from back to front.

A little while after Mitch and the agent finished hooking up the animals, the two stagecoach employees strolled back, the driver moving to inspect the traces.

"Passengers sure a fussy bunch," Cooley said.

"We've heard it all before," Sutton responded with a roll of his eyes.

"Ellsworth, is it?" Cooley directed his question to Mitch. "Ain't that something like the same name as one of them fellers who got shot up in a bank holdup some time ago back in Missouri?"

Mitch was prepared and nodded. "Same last name— might even be a distant cousin. Heard *that* Ellsworth was shot dead and buried." He gave the man his best grin. "You got any horse thieves among your kin?"

For a few seconds the man didn't know if he had been joshed or insulted. Finally he returned the grin. "Matter of fact, it jes' might be so."

"Much traffic on the road this morning?" Mitch posed his question to both men.

"Not much coming this way," the driver said. "Had a few riders went scooting 'round us."

"What sort of riders?" Mitch asked, thinking of Carlin's gang.

The driver gave him a questioning look. "Well, there was that one bunch of scruffy ones what looked like they had a mad on, but a few others were pleasant enough. Had those who gave us some 'howd-do's as they passed by." He paused. "Why you ask? Looking for someone special?"

"No, just making conversation, I guess," Mitch said.

As the passengers emerged from the station house to board the stage, the two men climbed back to their high seats and waved their farewells, the driver cracking the whip to prod the fresh team off to a jolting start.

"Too late for you to head out," Gilchrist said, watching the stagecoach diminish in size as it traveled into the distance. "Best spend the night, get some rest, and be off to a fresh start in the morning."

"Lots of daylight left," Mitch countered, and he gave a wry smile. "I suspect, Ed, that you need some company."

The station agent returned the smile and nodded his agreement. "Wish I had me a wife," he said. "Had one once, but she's dead more'n ten years now."

"You might marry again."

Gilchrist shrugged. "She was a pretty one, and I guess it spoiled me for any other." He shrugged again. "If I did find me a pretty lady, she surely wouldn't fancy an old coot like me."

"Well, not around here, I suppose," Mitch said. "But you might move into some town and give the local ladies a chance at you. Some might not be so pretty, but there are likely some passable widows who'd fancy a sturdy fellow like yourself."

"I've had that thought myself," Gilchrist agreed. "Keep hanging on here, though Lord knows why. Least you can have a late lunch or early supper with me."

"Might be the smart thing to do." Mitch laughed. "Lord knows when I'll get a decent meal again."

They entered the house and sat at the table for a half hour, the lunch consisting of leftovers from the food prepared for the stage passengers.

As the afternoon sunlight took on a noticeable slant, Mitch rose and stretched. "I guess I'd better be on my way," he said. "I do thank you for your hospitality."

"Glad for your company, young feller. Come back this way again—it'd be my pleasure." He reached into his hip pocket and, from a worn-slick leather wallet, counted out several dollar bills. "Here, something to help you on your way."

Mitch, with an impatient gesture, stepped back. "That's way too much, Ed," he protested. "For a day's work—"

"Pay me back if you ever get the chance, and, if you don't, do the same for some other fellow."

"I can't—"

"It'll be hard feelings if you don't let me do a good deed," Gilchrist persisted. "And that's a fact."

Mitch stood very still for some time and finally gave a short nod. "A loan it'll be," he said. "I'm short of cash, and that *is* a fact. But you'll get it back, every penny of it."

They shook hands, and Mitch walked to the shed and saddled his horse. He stepped into the stirrup and swung astride Belle, reflecting that such an effort was much easier now. The pain in his side had not completely gone away—it was more of a discomfort now with an occasional twinge of severity—but he could tell he was healing.

He tapped his boot heels into the mare's flanks, urging her into a trot, and, as he passed the station house, he waved again to the agent standing at the door. *Lonely guy,* he thought sympathetically. *The man needs companionship, winsome or plain—someone to share his life.*

A smile came to his face. "Or maybe I'm thinking what's good for him is more about me," he said aloud. Again he tapped his boot heels against Belle's flanks and nodded in satisfaction as she responded with a gallop. He let have her head for a half mile before reining her to a slower pace, patting her, and leaning into her ear to whisper his approval and affection. "Good girl."

An hour later he glanced back and saw a horseback rider at a distance. Believing that any adversary would be ahead rather than behind him, he thought nothing of another traveler on the road. But something nagged at him, and he reined Belle to a halt and turned in the saddle once again. The rider's horse was now coming at a gallop, and he recognized the heavyset man bouncing in the saddle. "Lord preserve us," he said in a low voice. "It's Pat McGrath, his very own self."

Three minutes later the younger McGrath reined up beside Mitch, his horse showing lather. "Howdy, Mitch!" he said in an exuberant greeting. "Fer a while there I thunk maybe I was on the wrong road."

"What in the Sam Hill are you doing here?" Mitch asked. "You run off from your folks?"

"Well, maybe from my ma, but my pa didn't say no," Pat said. "I jes tol' 'em that you was alone, and we figgered the rest of that bunch was tailing you and Bob going along this route. I figgered you might get yourself kilt 'less'n you had some help, so I followed them following you."

"Get down and rest your horse," Mitch said with a sigh. "I'm more afraid of getting killed by your ma if anything happens to you."

Both men dismounted and let their horses graze by the side of the lane while they found shade under a scrawny tree. They talked for fifteen minutes, Pat mostly justifying his supportive mission. They remounted and guided their horses onto the road toward the Red River.

"You ever been out of Arkansas?" Mitch asked as they rode side by side.

"Nope, first time."

"You've got no business doing this," Mitch reprimanded him. "It's my fault for bringing my troubles to your family."

"I'da been kilt a long time ago by that devil cat," Pat reminded him. "Let's jes' call this my way of getting square."

"Well, I guess it'd be nice to have traveling company," Mitch said reluctantly. "Let's mount up and cover some more miles before sunset."

"Pa did say one thing."

Mitch waited to hear.

"For me to mind what you tol' me and don't be stupid on my own."

Mitch broke into a hearty laugh and wagged his head back and forth in his mirth. "Lordy, kid, your old man has plumb forgot how yours truly is the one with a history of doing stupid things. Heaven knows, maybe there's a brain between the pair of us."

Chapter Eighteen

It was late in the day, just before dusk, as Mitch and Pat rode slowly down the central street of Sherman, Texas. Mitch swept his gaze from side to side, searching the boardwalks in front of the false-front buildings. He really did not expect to see Bob Carlin strolling along the avenue. He was quite aware that his quarry might be anyplace in the West, but Sherman was his best guess. After his first winter stay in the Texas community, Bob had often bragged of his decision to travel south and stay here with the other guerillas. He had been enthralled with the wild fun and carnal pleasures of this wide-open town.

Now, as the two traversed the central avenue, Mitch was searching for establishments that sold comfort or pleasure, the fancier the better. Unless Bob had changed a lot over the years, the money he had stolen from the bank and from his own followers would be burning a hole in his pocket. For him it would be the best hotel in town, the swankiest saloon, the brothel with the prettiest women—those were the establishments where Mitch would likely find his former comrade.

"We need to buy a little traveling food," Mitch said, nodding his head toward a grocery store. "It's not for sure we'll find Bob here in town, but we'll need supplies for the road back whether we do or not."

"Horses need some caring too," Pat said. "You got money for feed?"

Mitch nodded. "Thanks to a nice man back at a stage station, I do have a bit. Maybe even enough that we can buy *us* a cooked meal this evening—that is, if it's not too pricey."

A huge smile appeared on Pat's young face. "That'd go good, you betcha."

Mitch guided Belle to the side of the road, and Pat turned his horse to follow. They dismounted, tied their mounts to a hitching rail, and entered the store. It was a narrow building with flour, sugar, cracker, and pickle barrels lined along the left wall, and, on the other side, a long counter fronted shelves stacked with canned fruits and vegetables. At the near end of the counter a variety of sweets—jawbreakers, red-and-white candy ribbons, licorice whips, peppermints, toffees, and assorted bonbons—were displayed in a glass-topped cabinet.

"Help you, young gents?" Behind the counter, a middle-aged store clerk, bespectacled and wearing an apron, greeted them. "Been traveling, I see."

Mitch nodded. "Yeah, we're trailing a bit of dust when we walk." His eyes swept the shelves. "No beating 'round the bush, we're long on needs and short on money. Need some coffee, some biscuits, some beans, a slab of cured bacon and jerky . . . and that'll have to do it."

"You fellows looking for work?" the clerk asked, and a dejected look came to his face. "Not much hiring going on around here."

Mitch shook his head. "Just moving through. You know a place that sets a decent supper plate for a reasonable sum?"

"My sister runs a café three doors down," the slender clerk told them. "You tell her I sent you, and tell her I said to do you right."

"We appreciate your kindness, sir," Mitch said. "Pleasure doing business with you."

The clerk moved about behind the counter, reaching to the shelves for the tins of coffee and beans. "I'll get the bacon from out back," he told them. "Be right back."

With the slim supply of food sacked and paid for, Mitch and Pat thanked the clerk and walked out to their tethered horses. They divided the groceries and placed the goods into their saddlebags. They walked their horses down a side street to a nearby livery and gave two quarters to the stable hand for a couple of buckets of crushed oats. They brushed down both mounts, watered and fed them, then walked them back to the main street and tied them at the rail in front of a small café.

"I surely could use a sitting-down meal," Patrick said.

Mitch examined the sum of his money and sighed, then opened the door to the little restaurant and stood aside for Pat to enter. "This may very well be the last one for quite a spell."

It was dark when they left the café and strolled, their hunger satisfied, to stand at the hitching rail. Belle raised her face for Mitch to rub the star on her forehead.

"I'm going to run some of the bars. You keep your eyes peeled for any sign of Bob or any of his bunch," Mitch instructed. "You'd recognize Bob, but it isn't likely he'd know you. He hasn't seen you full grown."

"I look like my pa, they say," Pat countered. "I'll just hang back in the shadows."

"Good thinking," Mitch agreed. He reached out again to Belle and gave her another comforting pat on the nose, then walked away to begin a search of the main-street saloons. One by one he entered, standing quietly and unobtrusively in shadowed areas, careful not to bring attention to himself as he scrutinized the patrons. He looked carefully at each customer at the bars and at the tables. Even with his now-substantial beard and mustache, he was taking no chances that Bob, when and if discovered, would recognize him. *Not likely to see and recognize someone he believed to be a dead man,* Mitch reflected.

After an hour he entered yet another saloon, wearily pushing through the café doors. The sizable tavern featured a long walnut bar along the left wall crowded with a scattering of businessmen in suits and cowboys in their working clothes. Two large beer barrels were centered behind the bar, and a pair of bartenders moved to and from the spigots, drawing schooners at a continual pace.

In the open spaces of the saloon, patrons sat at eight round tables, three more at the back where poker games were conducted by professional gamblers. Five women in bright, colorful costumes circulated among the tables, pausing to chat with customers. A stairway at one side of the building led to an upper-story overlook where two men with shotguns sat with an overview of the activities below. Behind them, a corridor entrance revealed a passageway to private rooms.

Mitch stood for several minutes to survey the swirl of boisterous revelers. He waited until one of the young, provocatively clad women, prettier than most and slender, came close. Her face was smooth above the rouge on her cheeks, yet makeup was not quite able to mask a purplish bruise above her left eye and extending under her brunet hair. With surprisingly good teeth, she gave him something more than a welcoming smile.

"May I ask you a question?" Mitch asked.

The young woman's smile became a knowing smirk.

"I'm looking for a friend of mine," he told her. "Fellow about my same size and age, handsome, with a head of reddish-brown hair."

"Why are you asking me?" she said impatiently, stepping back, recognizing rejection.

"You're the prettiest girl in the place," Mitch told her. "You'd be the one he'd notice."

The young woman brought back part of her smile. "Maybe you outta tell me something more about him."

"Well, I'd say he's probably a big spender."

She gave Mitch a critical, appraising look, her eyes traveling over his trail-worn clothing. "You a big spender too?"

"Hardly," Mitch responded.

Her eyes met his, her manner cool. "If I did have some notion of this pal of yours, you'd make it worth my while?"

Mitch shook his head and managed a reluctant grin. "If I had it to give, I surely would, but . . ." He shrugged and began to walk away. "Guess I'll keep on asking around."

"Wait a minute," the young woman said. "Fella like that's been in the last couple of nights. Redheaded fella your size, like you said, showing a wad when he shouldn't." She suddenly seemed self-conscious. "Spent some on me, but he warn't at all nice about it."

Mitch came back to her. "His name Bob?"

She nodded. "He was fun at first."

Mitch gave considerable thought to his next statement. "He used to be a fun sort of a fellow, but he isn't anymore." He paused. "And about his being my friend . . . well, that's not exactly true any longer."

"He roughed me up a bit," she said, touching the bruise at her temple. "Still, I ain't one to be getting him killed or into bad trouble just to get even. Is that what you're fixing to do?"

"He got himself into trouble," Mitch told her. "Years ago and then again just lately."

"You the law or something?"

Mitch made his answer evasive. "I'm not here to kill him, so don't worry about that." He paused. "I *am* here to take him back to Missouri, where he's done some bad things."

"What bad things?"

"Taking things that didn't belong to him and . . . and roughing up people while he was taking what belonged to them."

She considered this information for a long while and then nodded. "You won't say I told on him?"

"For what you might believe my word is worth, you've got it," Mitch assured her. "Where can I find him?"

"Try the hotel a block up the street," she said. After a brief hesitation, she added, "Room nine."

With a nod of thanks, he turned and headed for the doorway. One of the café doors slammed into his chest, knocking him to one side as a cluster of ruffians bulled their way into the saloon. When the leader paused and gave him a malicious, challenging glance, Mitch recognized him immediately. *Carlin's man, Nate!*

"You figgering on bracing me, barfly?" the surly outlaw snarled.

"No, sir, sorry I got in your way," Mitch mumbled.

The outlaw started to move on, then hesitated and returned his gaze to Mitch, his stare intense. "I know you from somewhere?"

"No, sir," Mitch feigned timidity and lowered his head, avoiding eye contact. "May I go out now?"

The man's lips curled in contempt, and, with a nod of his head, he signaled his hooligans to follow. They crossed the room, swaggering their way to the bar, brushing and bumping young and old men out of their way.

I don't have enough problems?

Taking a deep breath, Mitch strode out of the barroom into the fading light of the evening. He walked down the boardwalk, and Pat emerged from the darkness to join him.

"You find him?"

"I think so," Mitch said, untying the reins from the rail. "Up the street at the hotel."

They walked, leading their horses along the main street to the two-story, white-painted clapboard hotel. Even from across the road, through a large front window, Mitch had a clear view of the lobby, and he could see a clerk sitting between a high counter and a wall-mounted rack of key and message pigeonholes.

"Take the horses back there to the stable and wait."

"Don't ya want me to go in with ya?"

Mitch shook his head. "I'd best do it alone."

Chapter Nineteen

Mitch had considered a bold approach: enter the foyer, mount the steps to the rooms, knock on the door of number nine, and take Bob by surprise. He quickly discarded that notion; the desk clerk would likely cause a commotion if Mitch did not provide a credible reason for barging in on someone.

After Pat led both horses to the hotel's small stable, Mitch stepped into a dark night shadow of a nearby building and stood very still, waiting for whatever opportunity might occur. From his concealed vantage point he watched the late-night traffic on the main street—occasional riders moving past and drunken revelers lurching homeward.

After a twenty-minute vigil, he saw the desk clerk rise, hurry into a dark corridor, and disappear from view.

A privy break! Mitch thought with elation. He trotted across the street and up the steps and eased through the front door, making sure not to make a noise. He walked quickly across the lobby to peer down the dark corridor to be sure the clerk was nowhere in sight, then he moved behind the desk, scanned the small message-box compartments, and snatched a spare key from the one marked with the number nine.

He hurried to the stairway and, taking two steps at a time, ascended to the upper floor. A wall-mounted oil lamp burning at low flame gave faint illumination to the second-story passageway, barely enough to reveal the brass numbers on the doors. Mitch walked softly to room number nine and leaned close to the door, his head nearly touching it, listening for sounds inside.

Although hearing nothing within, Mitch tried the knob cautiously, then inserted the key and turned it as quietly as possible. He drew his Colt revolver, cocked it, and eased the door open just enough to slip inside.

Nobody here!

He holstered his revolver, closed the door, and stood still for a few moments to let his eyes adjust to the dimness. Then he swept his gaze around the room. It was of modest size with a double bed and a night table beside it, a washstand with a mirror on the wall above it, and a chest of drawers next to the closet door. He stepped to the highboy and opened each of the drawers, finding all of them empty. He looked next in the closet and, feeling along the floor in the dark interior, found a set of leather saddlebags. He pulled it out, opened one fat pocket, then the other, and nodded his satisfaction. "The bank money," he whispered. "Bob, you damned fool, hotel's got to have a safe," he continued with a shake of his head. "Left in the room for any sneak thief to take while you're out partying."

He considered his options. A great temptation was to walk away with the money. He could return it to the bank in Harrisonville, declare his innocence, as demonstrated by the money's recovery, and, with luck, the collaborating testimony of the Jennings woman. On the other hand, he might still be arrested and tried as a member of the band of outlaws. His return of the money could be considered as merely a ruse to avoid a long jail sentence or even hanging. And the people who had helped him might also be punished for their aid and alleged duplicity. *Maybe I should take the money and head for Mexico or South America,* he thought, then shrugged the notion away.

His thoughts were abruptly interrupted by a loud commotion from the floor below, shouts and swearing voices rising. With a sense of looming danger, Mitch slung the saddlebags over his shoulder, strode swiftly to the door, and let himself out into the hallway. He walked softly to the top of the stairs, staying well within the shadows to peer down into the hotel lobby. His hunch was verified; the frightened desk clerk was cowering behind the counter as Bob Carlin was being dragged by two of his former henchmen toward the stairway. Behind them, the rest of the outlaw gang was jostling for space inside the front door.

"We want the money!" the group's new leader, Nate, bellowed as he walked ahead of the prisoner. "Every nickel of it, or you're a dead man!" He swung a fist at Carlin's already battered face and followed it with a blow to the stomach.

"It's in the room," Carlin muttered through swollen lips. "In the closet."

"It better be!" another ruffian brayed.

Mitch stepped back and retreated along the hallway as Carlin's captors began to drag him up the steps. Mitch looked around anxiously, realizing he would be totally exposed when the men reached the second floor. Behind him, at the end of the corridor, he spotted a window and moved quickly toward it. To his relief, it opened easily, and, as he had hoped, he found the steel-grate platform of the hotel's fire escape outside. He tossed the saddle-bags onto the platform and slipped through the opening. He lowered the window, leaving an inch-high space open at the bottom. He lay flat on the slatted metal rods of the platform and peered back into the corridor, believing the darkness of the night and his position would hide him from anything other than a searching view. Although acutely aware of the risk he was taking by remaining, he was intrigued by the drama unfolding before him. With some chagrin, he realized he was actually worried about the fate of Carlin, his former friend.

The agitated huddle of angry outlaws came to the upper level, hauling Carlin toward his room, as their leader, Nate, strode ahead to turn the knob and open the door. The two men, dragging Carlin between them, propelled him into the room as the others crowded in behind him.

"Where is it?" Nate's voice was loud.

"In the closet," came the muffled reply. "Saddlebags're on the floor."

There was a short period of scuffling noise followed by a string of oaths. "It ain't here! Where'd you hide it, you lying cur?" Nate barked.

"Maybe it's under the bed!" another voice said. "Look there!"

A few more moments went by with muted sounds of the search, and again Nate shouted his fury. "Damn you, Bob Carlin! It ain't here! Tell me where it is, or I'll kill you dead right here!"

"It's gotta be here." Carlin's voice was husky and tinged with disbelief. "Right in there on the floor."

In the hallway, Mitch could see that two doors had been cracked open, fearful room occupants peering out, alarmed at the violent commotion. Then the raucous utterances from room nine suddenly ceased and turned to ominous silence. Mitch heard the cocking of a revolver.

"Wait a minute!" came Carlin's frantic cry. "You're right—I got it hid! You kill me, and you'll never find it."

The silence lasted for several long moments. "You got it here? Maybe down in the hotel safe?"

"No, not here," Carlin declared blearily. "I'll tell you where if you let me go."

"He's lying," one of the outlaws said. "Trying to save his hide."

"You can have it all," Carlin persisted. "I'm done with it. Just take it, and give me my life—that's all I can ask."

"Kill him, Nate!" someone said. "We'll find it."

"Hold on," Nate said. "Bob, here, is doing the right thing. Bob, you take us to where you got the money hid, and we'll let you go."

"When you get the money, you'll shoot me," Carlin countered, his voice ragged with pain and fear. "You gotta give me a chance if you ever hope to see any of that cash."

"We'll get it outta him," still another outlaw's voice threatened. "Two of you go downstairs to watch the doors while we work it out of him!"

Mitch, being careful not to make sound, crawled across the fire escape to a short set of steps that descended to a swing-down stairway locked in its upper position. He realized that lowering it to the ground would cause considerable noise and bring Carlin's captors on the run. Instead, shouldering the saddlebags, he moved down the three steps and climbed over the railing, his booted feet between the stair's wide-spaced stanchions. Moving as quietly as possible, he stooped and looked down to gauge the distance to the ground. In the darkness it was difficult to see, but it appeared to be a drop of ten feet, maybe more. He searched in the gloom for anything below that could cause an injury, but the area seemed clear of any protruding dangers. He slipped the saddle-bags from his shoulder and, bending as low as possible, swung the joined pouches and released the pair. To his satisfaction, the leather bags soared out and landed with a soft plop, scarcely a sound to his ears and certainly not to those of anyone on the second floor of the hotel.

He reached down to grasp the base of the platform, swung himself over, and hung for a few moments until his body's swaying stilled. Then he opened his hands and dropped, flexing his knees to absorb the shock of the fall. Even so, the impact was a jolt to his body, hammering pain into his still-sore torso. He lay on the ground and waited for the throbbing to subside, for a few terrible moments fearing that he had torn something loose. A second fear possessed him: he wondered if he had cried out, and he cursed himself for leaving the window above partially opened. *Could they have heard my outcry? Did I make one?*

A minute or two passed, and suddenly a dark hulk moved above him. Mitch stabbed his hand to his holster but abruptly froze the motion. "Pat?"

The dark silhouette's head nodded, and the bulky figure stooped down. "You okay?" the young man asked. "I saw you jump down. What's going on?"

Mitch sat up gingerly and then struggled to his feet. He walked to retrieve the saddlebags and laid them over his shoulder. "We missed getting here by a day, maybe even by a couple of hours," he said in a low voice, and he nodded at the hotel. "Bob's gang caught up with him."

"They're up there now?" Pat asked anxiously. "They kill him?"

"Not yet," Mitch told him. "They're busting him up to tell them where the loot from the bank is."

"Ain't he got it?"

"Nope," Mitch said, tapping a pouch of the saddlebags. "I've got it."

Even in the dark Mitch could see the grin appear on the young man's face. "Hey, ain't that whatcha come after? To get the money back to the bank?"

"Well, that might be of some help," Mitch admitted. "Be better to bring the money *and* the head thief."

"You mean Bob? Why bother? Ain't that bunch of hooligans gonna put his name on a headstone?"

"Well, I was thinking of somehow getting him loose," Mitch said.

"Well, if that don't beat all," Pat exclaimed. "How many of 'em got him?"

"Five or six—I'm not sure." He shrugged. "I don't think they'll kill him just yet," Mitch said. "They're all upset about the money, and from what I overheard, Bob's playing for time, telling them he can take them to the cash."

"How you figgering to outdo them outlaws?"

Mitch frowned deep in thought. "What we need is a diversion."

"A what?"

"Something to distract them," Mitch said. He opened the flap of one pouch, reached inside, and brought out a wrapper-banded sheaf of bills. He tore off the band and handed the money to Pat. "Here, go to the nearest saloon, start passing out some greenbacks to the shady ladies there, and tell them there's a lot more to be had at the hotel. Tell them to go to room nine."

Pat's face showed his puzzlement.

"And then, soon as you see any of those Jezebels going in the hotel, you go to *next* bar and tell all the toughest rowdies you can find that up in room nine, there's some nasty hombres mistreating and hurting the very flower of Sherman, Texas, womanhood."

Pat gave a delighted chuckle. "And what if I spread the word that there's a fire at hotel too—how about that?"

"That's another good idea. That ought to bring the fire wagon, the volunteers, and a whole lot of people wanting to watch."

"What are you going to be doing?" Patrick asked.

"I'll sort that out when the fun begins," Mitch told him. "Better get a move on. They might be fixing to kill old Bob any minute now."

Pat gave a nod and a wave of his hand. "Be back in a jiffy."

Chapter Twenty

Five minutes later, Mitch saw a small group of saloon women in garish dresses hurrying toward and then entering the hotel. And, only a few minutes later, to his satisfaction and amusement, a fast-striding cluster of nearly a dozen men appeared in the middle of the street, anger in their aggressive motions and boisterous voices. Adding to the dissonance, the urgent ringing of a distant bell signaled a fire alarm.

Even from outside the hotel he could hear the escalation of shouts and screams coming from inside the building. He walked to the front entrance and paused as the breathless young McGrath hurried to join him.

"Did I do good?" Pat panted.

"Sounds like a real donnybrook going on," Mitch said with an approving nod.

"Now what?"

"Wait 'til the fire wagon comes," Mitch said. "We need a mite more confusion."

"Well, we ain't gonna wait long—here she comes!"

Mitch turned to see a group of young men propelling a pump wagon toward the hotel. With four pulling at the front and a half dozen more pushing from the back, they brought it to a stop at the curb adjacent to the hotel's entrance. "Where's the fire?" one young man shouted.

"Second floor!" Mitch called out. "Way at the back!"

The volunteer firefighters heaved the pump wagon over the curb and positioned it on the lawn next to the front porch. Two of the men began to unwind the long hose, dragging it up and across the porch and into the hotel foyer. Townspeople were now swarming along the street, hurrying toward the hotel, eager to witness the excitement of a conflagration.

"You fellows!" Mitch shouted. "They need you inside!"

A surge of more than twenty men ran toward the doors, arms waving, shouting for others to follow.

"Let's go," Mitch said, and he started running, mingling with the invading horde. Pat lagged only a couple of seconds before he began lumbering in pursuit.

Inside, the scene was bedlam, men on the ground floor pushing and shoving toward the stairway, their sheer numbers blocking the floundering pumpwagon volunteers in their efforts to deploy the fire hose. There were fistfights on the stairway. At the top of the steps two saloon women were clawing at each other's hair while one young hero with an angry, buxom female over his shoulder tried to find a path to the lobby.

"Up the stairs," Mitch said as Pat joined him. "Room nine."

Pat took the lead, his heavy bulk blasting through the struggling figures on the staircase, Mitch following in his wake. On the second floor, the bullish rush of the young man took them to the open door of room nine. Inside, Mitch spotted three of the outlaws vainly trying to defend themselves not only from male assailants but also from the kicks and fingernail slashes of two furious bar girls.

Slumped in a chair near the door, Bob Carlin appeared to be nearly unconscious, his clothes in disarray, his face showing cuts and welts. Mitch moved to him, bent down, and slung him over his shoulder in a fireman's carry. "Lead the way!" he shouted to Pat.

As they moved out into the corridor, Pat started toward the staircase and then stopped. The hallway was jammed with men and women and a crush of many more forcing their way up.

"This ain't no good," Pat said, turning to Mitch.

"This way," Mitch said, beckoning as he carried Carlin to the window at the end of the hall. "Fire escape."

Mitch opened the window and, with Pat crawling through first, they maneuvered the barely conscious gang leader out and onto the grated platform. Mitch moved through the window and closed it as Pat unlocked the hinged stairs and lowered the stairway.

"What's happening?" Carlin said groggily.

"We're saving your life," Mitch growled, and he hoisted him once again to his shoulder. He descended the steps, and once on the ground with his dazed burden, he picked up Carlin's saddlebags and hurried to the nearby stable, Pat trotting along beside him. Mitch slung the money-filled saddlebags in front of his saddle horn. He opened a pouch of his own saddlebags, took out the manacle, and then moved on.

"We need his horse," Mitch said as they entered the shed. "I think it's that bay over there." He propped the groaning Carlin against a support post and entered the bay's stall. "Keep an eye on Carlin while I strap on the saddle," he instructed.

"He's in no shape to be going nowhere," young McGrath said.

In less than two minutes Mitch had the saddle on the horse and the bridle bit in its mouth. "Help me get him on."

Together, they heaved the unconscious man into the saddle, where he slumped forward and leaned precariously to one side.

"What's to keep him from falling off?" Pat asked.

By way of answer, Mitch wrapped the chain of the manacle around the saddle horn and snapped the cuffs onto Carlin's wrists. "He may tilt this way and that, but this ought to hold him," Mitch speculated. "Let's move!"

Once he and Pat sat their own mounts, they rode closely on either side of the unconscious man to keep him from falling. As they rode away, they could see that the hotel melee continued unabated, with more and more citizens involved.

Minutes later, well past the outskirts of the settlement, Mitch and Pat turned their mounts to the right to lead their inert captive's horse far from the road. They entered a grove of trees and, in the deep darkness of the woods, found a clearing. "How's he doing?" Mitch asked.

Pat bent to examine Carlin. "Looks pretty banged up. Reckon it'd do him some good to rest a spell."

"Keep an eye on him while I gather some wood and make a fire."

"Any chance his gang followed us?"

"I don't think so," Mitch said from the cluster of the surrounding trees. "I've been keeping a close eye behind us." After a few minutes he emerged from the copse, his arms cradling a load of brushwood. "I'll get the fire started, and then I'll help you get him down."

Thirty minutes later Carlin came to and began to question his circumstances. "What's happening?" he muttered through swollen lips. He tried to sit up and discovered the handcuffs binding him. "Damn it, what's this?"

"I liked it better when he was out cold," Patrick said.

"Same old bad temper," Mitch observed. "I guess the beating didn't really addle his brain."

Carlin looked back and forth at the men sitting on the other side of the small open fire. "Who in tarnation are you two?"

"You might call us your guardian angels," Mitch offered. "Rescued you from that bunch of cuthroats beating on you."

Carlin lifted the manacle. "Why you got me shackled?" he demanded. "You the law? Bounty hunters or something?"

"Something," Mitch said.

"You the ones that took my money?"

"*Your* money? There's a bank up in Harrisonville that thinks it's *their* money."

"And now you're planning to make it yours," Carlin countered. "You're just another couple of—"

"Thieves?" Mitch questioned sarcastically. "Yeah, we've got it. Foolish of you to leave it lying around while you were out carousing."

Carlin's eyes searched the dark figure, puzzlement in his voice. "You haven't said who you are, but you sound like somebody I . . ." He didn't continue.

"Somebody you knew?"

"Somebody you couldn't be."

Mitch turned to him in the faint light. "It's Mitch, old friend."

Carlin's face showed shock and disbelief as he stared at the bearded man. His eyes widened as he attempted to speak, then clamped shut as he shuddered and shook his head.

"You should've finished me yourself, Bob," Mitch said calmly. "You ought to have known that Hubie had a soft heart."

Carlin opened his eyes in wonderment with a stare that lasted for a long time. Finally he dropped his gaze. "For a while there I thought I was hearing a ghost." He shook his head slowly. "Guess saying I'm sorry isn't going to do any good, will it?"

"None at all."

Carlin turned his gaze to the other man, trying to make out his face in the flickering firelight. "This can't be big Luke McGrath, can it?"

"Howdy, Bob," Pat interrupted. "Been a long time since I last seed ya."

Carlin looked closely at the hefty young man. "You that McGrath pup grown to size?" He shook his head. "You're a danged fool, mixing in this business. You never had a lick of sense as a tyke, and seems growing up didn't help."

"Shut up, Bob," Mitch interjected.

"You gonna kill me?"

"Maybe."

"Look, just let me go. You take the money, and—"

"We could've walked away with the money long ago, but that's not what I'm after."

Carlin remained silent for a long time before, at last, he spoke. "Well, then, get on with it. All I ask is, make it a head shot, not in the gut."

"The gut's where you shot me, Bob," Mitch reminded him. "Still hurts."

Carlin shrugged. "I don't suppose I've got the right, but, for old time's sake—"

"Doing 'old time's sake' for you was almost the death of me."

"Well, if you ain't going to kill me, what then?" Carlin asked.

"That man shot down in the Harrisonville bank—did you do that?"

Carlin shook his head. "No, that was Nate . . . Nathan Roby." He paused. "You were right about that young skunk—he's no good, nothing but a hothead. He just hauled off and shot that poor fellow without any reason. No reason at all."

"I'm taking you back to Missouri," Mitch said. "We return the money, and you turn yourself in."

"And why would I do that?" Carlin gave a snort of contempt. "I'd be heading for a hanging, and you know it."

"Maybe not," Mitch countered. "You take your chances that they'll jail you only for the robbery and not for the murder."

Carlin's gaze swept from Mitch to Pat and back again. "It's a long way between here and Harrisonville. Just the two of you?" He laughed.

Mitch tossed another small branch onto the fire and watched until it smoldered and then flared to brighten the other flames. "We'll give you some rest 'til first light. Like you say, it's a long way back."

Chapter Twenty-one

On the second day out of Sherman, they covered nearly thirty miles, Mitch and Pat riding side by side with their prisoner a few feet ahead of them. They remained on the main road heading back to Arkansas, occasionally passing or meeting other travelers on horseback or driving wagons. Only two travelers noticed the manacle—one cuff on Carlin's right wrist, the other clasped tightly around his saddle horn. Both men, although giving questioning looks, moved on without comment.

"Nice of you to let me tote the money," Carlin said in sarcasm, glancing at the saddlebags behind him.

"You stole it. You might as well enjoy carrying it." Then Mitch asked, "Spend much of it?"

"Not much. There's still about twenty-two thousand,

maybe a little more," Carlin answered. "Look, Mitch, you've got to believe me—I did feel bad about what I did back there. I wish I hadn't—"

"Of course you felt bad," Mitch cut in. "And the shot to the head to finish me—you were sorry about that too?"

Carlin's mouth tightened into a thin line. "One way or another, I'm gonna get loose."

"Thanks for the warning." Mitch voiced his sarcasm. "We'll take extra care."

"There'll be a time when you won't."

They rode on in silence, traversing a long, straight stretch with no other travelers in sight. As the sun's edge touched the far horizon and they approached a heavily forested area, Mitch rode his horse close to Carlin's bay, grasping the crown of the bridle to steer both animals from the road and head them deep into the woods, with Pat trailing behind.

"What are you up to now?" Carlin questioned.

"Figured you might be getting a little saddle sore," Mitch said cheerfully. "Maybe you could use a good stretch while Pat and I fix up some supper."

He reined his horse to a stop, his eyes looking upward, examining the surrounding trees. "This'll do fine." He released his grip on the bridle, swung down from his mount, and tied the reins to the slender bole of a tree. "Cover him, Pat," he instructed. Young McGrath drew his sidearm, cocked it, and aimed it at the outlaw. Mitch nodded his satisfaction and walked to the side of his

captive's horse. "Don't try anything. I'm going to unlock the cuff."

Carlin sighed, his face grim with anger as he watched
Mitch insert the key in the lock of the saddle horn cuff.
As it came loose, Carlin stretched out from the saddle
and, with his right hand free, whipped the chain at
Mitch's head.

Mitch was nimble in stepping back, wearing a smile of
amusement as the open cuff end of the manacle missed
him by more than two feet. "I figured you'd have to try,"
he said easily, and he drew his revolver.

"Your hillbilly didn't shoot," Carlin said, his lips tightly
pursed. "And I figured he wouldn't."

"He will next time," Mitch said in a raised voice.
"Pat, any kind of a sudden move he makes, you do it, no
hesitation." He brandished his own Colt. "Get down
slowly, and walk ahead of me."

Swearing under his breath, Carlin stepped down from
his horse and, with a glare, turned his back to Mitch.

"Walk to that tree about ten feet ahead," Mitch instructed. He followed Carlin as the outlaw, with the
manacle dangling from his right wrist, moved to a
medium-seized red oak with a leafy canopy above and a
spread of lower limbs. "That's good," Mitch said. "Now
reach up and snap that cuff around that lower branch."

"No," Carlin said, shaking his head. "You're not going
chain me up like a—"

"Do it, Bob," Mitch cut in. He made a slashing motion

with his revolver. "Unless you want to be pistol-whipped again."

For a few moments Carlin stared his defiance and then, angrily, reached up and placed the open cuff around the branch.

"Snap it nice and tight."

There were a few seconds more of noncompliance before Carlin shrugged and closed the cuff around the branch.

Mitch walked behind the outlaw, reached for and tested the cuff's closure. Satisfied, he holstered the Colt and walked away to take the reins of Carlin's bay in his hand and led the animal to where his mare was tied. Patrick swung down from his saddle and tied his horse with the other two. In a few seconds the noses of all three animals were down as they grazed on grass.

"You gonna leave me hung up like this all night?" Carlin snarled.

"You're the one who keeps bragging about how you're going to get clear of us," Mitch said with a sidelong merry glance at Pat. "Even so, we might let you down when the food's ready."

"Mighty kind of you," Carlin groused.

For the next quarter hour Mitch and Pat built a small fire and, from their meager rations, prepared a pot of coffee and a skimpy meal of beans, beef jerky, and hardtack. With Pat standing a couple of yards away with a drawn revolver, Mitch unlocked the cuff from the branch and then, pulling his own Colt from his holster, motioned Carlin to the fire.

"Can I take this damned thing off?" Carlin asked as he rubbed his wrist under the cuff. "I'm rubbed clear raw."

"Comes from trying to pull out of it," Mitch countered. "Hook yourself up again, both hands."

"How'll I eat?"

"You'll manage."

Grumbling, Carlin cuffed his left wrist and, at the fireside, sat down with a string of oaths leveled at his captors. Mitch and Carlin ate first, Pat standing guard with his pistol aimed directly at the outlaw. When they finished, Mitch took the guard duty to allow young McGrath his meal.

"This how it's going to work tonight?" Carlin asked. "Taking turns watching me while the other one sleeps?"

"Maybe we'll jest hook you back to that there tree and see how you doze standing up," Pat said with a mischievous smile. "How'd that be?"

"Watch your mouth, you backwoods lunkhead!" Carlin said gruffly.

"We'll work out your sleeping arrangement when bedtime comes," Mitch said calmly.

"Better drink lots of that coffee to stay awake," Carlin jeered. "When I see one of you drooping, that'll be all I need."

Neither Mitch nor Pat responded to his threat.

"I've been meaning to ask," the captive asked. "How'd you track me?"

"You've always been predictable in your ways, Bob," Mitch answered. "And you always did talk a lot," he told him. "I recalled your saying something about heading south, and I just guessed it might be Texas, a place you've always had a hankering for." He reached down for a small branch and tossed it onto the fire, sparks flying up at the impact. "I expect you shot off your mouth to that wild bunch of yours as well. I'd guess that's what brought them along."

Carlin jerked his manacled hands at Pat. "How'd you hook up with the kid? You were down in Arkansas with his clan?"

Mitch nodded.

"You was planning to take me right in the middle of all my boys and the Jessup clan?"

Again Mitch nodded. "We were set to do it while you were fishing upstream by yourself."

Carlin chuckled. "Never saw you or nobody, but I had kind of a hunch, like maybe there was somebody near. Lucky I took off."

"Just made the job harder."

"Job's not over yet."

Mitch took a sip of coffee from his tin cup and made a face. "Cold," he said. He arose from the ground, stepped to the fire, and poured out the contents of the cup. "Best we start thinking about some shut-eye." He walked into the darkness and, after a few seconds, returned to stand behind Carlin, holding something next to his body. "I'll need your help, Pat."

Carlin's head swiveled to look back at Mitch, and, apprehensive, he started to rise. "What are you—"

Mitch shoved the prisoner back to the ground as Pat came around the fire. "Hold him down, Pat. I'm going to help him get a good night's sleep."

"The hell you are!" Carlin managed to shout before Pat threw his heavy body over the man. "Get off, you dumb ox!"

"Got him?" Mitch asked as he knelt beside them.

Young Pat put all his weight on the struggling man's torso, pinning his manacled hands between their bodies. With his hard-muscled arms, he pressed big hands down on Carlin's shoulders to immobilize any movements other than a bobbing head and fluttering feet.

Mitch brought the bottle of laudanum tincture into view. He unscrewed the cap and poured it level to the brim. Placing the open bottle securely upright between his knees, he placed his left hand over Carlin's eyes and nose. "Open wide, Bob," he coaxed. "A little sleeping potion."

Under his hand, Carlin's head tried to move, and his lips tightened into a thin line. Mitch increased the downward pressure and, with his thumb and index finger, pinched the nose and closed the nostrils. There was a furious grunt, and, after a few stubborn seconds, the mouth came open, and Mitch poured the capful of liquid inside and quickly shifted his hand to keep the lips closed.

As soon as he saw Carlin swallow, he released his grip and reached again for the laudanum bottle.

"Mitch!" Carlin sputtered. "What did you give me? Poison?"

"You were wondering how we were going to keep watch over you," Mitch said calmly as he poured a second capful. "As the lady told me, this ought to keep you pretty doped up. Open wide."

Mitch repeated the action and, as he watched the second dose go down, he rose and recapped the bottle. "You can let him up now, Pat," he said. "Pleasant dreams, Bobby."

Pat rolled away and came to his feet as Carlin pushed up from the ground in a furious leap, rage on his face as he whirled first to the burly young man and then to Mitch. "You danged, dirty . . . I'll kill you with my bare hands!" He lunged and swung his cuffed hands at Mitch's head, the arc of his miss throwing him off balance as Mitch stepped away. When he clumsily regained his footing and spun to renew the attack, he stumbled and veered in his charge, staggering toward Pat.

"Don't let him fall into the fire," Mitch said mildly.

Carlin came to a teetering stop and swayed, then began to sag. Patrick stepped forward to catch him under the armpits before the outlaw fell facedown into the burning embers.

He dragged him a few feet away. "What do I do with him?" the young man asked.

"Just lay him down on that smooth patch right there," Mitch instructed. "We'll get a blanket over him for the night."

Pat gently positioned the inert body on the ground, looking to make sure there were no pebbles or exposed tree roots beneath him. He bent closely to study Carlin's face. "You think you maybe killed him?"

"Maybe, maybe not," Mitch replied. "Never took more than one capful myself." He walked to stand over the motionless outlaw. "We'll see how he is in the morning."

Chapter Twenty-two

Carlin came awake slowly and in an obvious debilitating haze. Fearful and confused, the outlaw twisted his head to look up and around at the sound of boots scuffing nearby, and with dim reason swimming back, anger flooded his expression. "Damn you! What did you—"

"Sleep well?" Mitch asked cheerfully. "We did."

"I didn't sleep at all," Carlin snarled as he shifted into a sitting position.

"Funny, I could swear I heard you snoring," Mitch countered. "Want some breakfast?"

"Breakfast?"

"Not much, I'll admit," Mitch said. "Same as supper. Beef jerky, coffee, and a biscuit or two, but it'll have to do." He looked closely at Carlin. "You feeling okay?"

"I feel terrible," Carlin mumbled. "What was that awful stuff?"

"Some pain medicine," Mitch answered, and he gestured to his side. "I lived on it for quite a spell, getting over the bullet hole you put in me."

Carlin shook his head, more to clear it than to react to Mitch's reproach. "You going to do this to me every night 'til we get to where we're going?"

Mitch gave a short laugh. "There's a stage station right up the road a piece. Maybe there we can arrange a different sleeping arrangement, at least for tonight."

"Keep this in mind," Carlin growled. "One day between here and Missouri, some way, you two are going to make mistakes. And I'm counting on it."

Mitch nodded. "I'll take your body slung over your bay if you want it that way, Bob. And *you* can count on *that*." He reached down to grip the chain between the handcuffs and tugged the captive to his feet, where the outlaw swayed. "You still look kinda unsteady. Let me help you over to the fire."

"You've turned damned hard, my old friend," Carlin said, weaving from side to side as Mitch pulled him along.

"And I'd say you gave me good cause," Mitch said with an edge in his voice. They walked a few yards to join Pat, who was tending to the coffeepot over a small fire.

"Sit down," Mitch said to Carlin. "Soon as we eat, we're in our saddles again."

Carlin slumped to the ground and wagged his head, trying to shake the cobwebs from behind his eyes. He looked up at Mitch, and a sad, remorseful expression came over his face. "Look, Mitch, you've got to understand. . . . It was me worrying about going back to jail that was the reason for what I did to you," Carlin said earnestly. "I know it was wrong, but you've got to understand that I was worried you'd tell and put me back in prison." He paused, his eyes searching Mitch's face. "Would you have told?"

"I can't say for sure."

"You see there? I wasn't exactly wrong, was I? You blaming me for making just that one bad mistake, and—"

"No, that won't cut it, Bob," Mitch broke in brusquely. "The plain truth is that you turned bad a long time back. I saw it beginning when we first started going against the law. Oh, I know, we told ourselves that the blasted Yankees were the cause of it, that we were only trying to take back what they took from us, but way down deep, I knew we were doing wrong." He grimaced. "I came to hate what I was doing, but I saw you take to it like a duck to water."

"We were doing what was right!" Carlin argued. "You just said it yourself—we were only taking back what we was due."

"Have it your way," Mitch said wearily. "You always have." He nodded at the nest of tin plates and the meager fare alongside. "Use your mouth for eating and not for excuse-making." Mitch reached for a cup and poured coffee into it. "Here," he said, offering the steaming cup to his prisoner. "Maybe it's hot enough to clear your brain."

By midafternoon, the trio came in sight of the stage station. They continued to ride until they turned in at the hardpan open area in front of the long adobe building. "We'll stop here for a chance to rest," Mitch said to Carlin. "I spent some time here on my way to find you."

They rode up to the hitching rail at the front of the building, where Mitch and Pat swung down from their horses, while Carlin sat chained to his saddle. "I hope Ed might see fit to fix us up with a half-decent meal."

"Can I get down?" Carlin asked crossly.

Before Mitch had a chance to answer, Ed Gilchrist stepped out of the front door and ambled toward them, his eyes darting first to the burly Pat McGrath and then fastening upon the manacled rider. "Well, well, well," he said with a sidelong glance at Mitch, "what in the world do we have here?"

"Caught up with my old pal," Mitch said with cheerful sarcasm, pointing at Carlin. "He's kinda putting up a fuss about going home to put some things back where they belong." He gave a nod to his burly companion. "This is a friend of mine, Patrick McGrath. He came along, joining up to help me." Mitch turned supplicant with his next question. "We've no right to stop here under these circumstances, and I'll certainly understand if you'd like us to move on, but . . ."

"I don't reckon there's any harm in your doing a stopover," Gilchrist said with a glance at Carlin. "Is he feeling okay?"

"Still a little woozy from some sleeping stuff I gave him," Mitch answered. "I expect he'll recover soon enough." He nodded to the front door. "I was wondering if we could get a meal. We can pay."

"Sure," Gilchrist agreed. "When she comes in, I'll have my Indian woman fix enough for us all." He inclined his head toward Carlin. "Gonna leave him on his horse?"

"I guess we can let him down long enough to eat," Mitch conceded. He walked to Carlin's horse and, warily, undid the cuff from the saddle horn.

Carlin slowly eased himself out of the saddle and stepped down to the ground. "You going to give me a break from this danged thing?" He paused. "Give you my word I won't try anything."

"There once was a Bob Carlin I believed," Mitch said in response. He walked to the outlaw's horse and removed the cash-filled saddlebags. "That fellow doesn't exist anymore."

Carlin and Mitch stared at each other for a long time, Ed Gilchrist's gaze switching back and forth to study each of them. Finally Carlin lowered his eyes, reached for the metal cuff, and snapped it tightly around his left wrist.

"C'mon in," Gilchrist said, and he led the trio to the door. "You all need to spend the night?"

"That's a lot to ask," Mitch said hesitantly as he ushered his prisoner into the station house. "If we did, you got an inside room with no windows and a door I can lock?"

"I got a couple of storerooms," Gilchrist replied. "Nothing in one of 'em 'cept some taters, flour, and cooking pots and pans."

"Any frying pans?" Carlin said with a crooked grin.

"We'll move that sort of weapon out before we lock you in for the night," Mitch said, a smile of remembrance touching his lips. "Just remember, we'll be right outside and sleeping light."

Chapter Twenty-three

The following morning, after the Chickasaw cook had cleaned up the kitchen and departed, the four men sat at the table in a surprisingly convivial conversation. Bob Carlin, still in handcuffs, made jokes about the difficulties of eating in the manacle and regaled the station agent with tales involving his own and Mitch's outlaw careers.

"We rode some with the James boys and, once, with Cole Younger," Carlin said, making sure to associate himself with the best-known bandit names. "Robbed a bank with Jesse down near Warrensburg, but we didn't get enough to pay more'n five or six dollars to each man." He glanced to Mitch for confirmation and accepted the faint smile and nod of agreement. "We did some better once we robbed a train."

"Made about fifteen hundred on that grand theft," Mitch put in with a roll of his eyes. "Split nine ways after Jesse took a thousand of it."

"Where'd you fit in?" the station agent asked Patrick. "You surely weren't old enough to go robbing trains and banks."

"No, sir," Pat said. "I was just a young'un when Mitch and Bob come to stay with us whilst all that was a-going on."

"We hid out in their neck of the woods," Carlin explained. "Pat's pa was with us in what was our part in the war, but not with the gangs later." He canted his head toward Mitch. "Big Luke—that's Patrick's old man—he and Mitch were kinda close."

"And what about you?" Gilchrist questioned.

"I guess I was too ornery for them," Carlin admitted. "Rubbed the family the wrong way, I'd say."

"Amen to that," Pat added.

"You boys did prison time?" Gilchrist inquired of Mitch and Carlin, lighting his corncob pipe for the fourth time, puffing hard in hopes of sustaining the tobacco ember in the bowl.

"Yes, sirree, we both paid our debts to society in full," Carlin said promptly.

"You still got more to pay," Mitch interposed. "Prison didn't make Bob any smarter."

"Well, I just didn't want to give up on my trade," Carlin countered with a merry smile. "I'd honed my skills and didn't want to waste 'em."

Mitch shrugged his affability away and didn't respond. He turned to Gilchrist. "Stage due today? I didn't see your helper around."

The agent shook his head. "Comes in tomorrow. Joseph only comes in when I need him."

"That storeroom sure was tight as a tick," Carlin said, and he brandished the cuffs on his wrists. "There was no reason for me to wear these while I was cooped up in there. I couldn't have busted through those mud brick walls, and that door is at least a couple inches thick." He shook his head. "No way I could've busted out."

"Get used to those cuffs. You'll be wearing them 'til we get home," Mitch said bluntly.

The station agent rose from the table and walked to the front door, looking at the slant of the morning sun beaming through the open front door and the adjacent window. "Getting on late in the day, danged near eight o'clock." He stepped outside, and they heard him knocking the cold tobacco residue from his pipe.

Mitch nodded and started to stand. "I need to take care of the horses."

"I'll do 'er," Pat said eagerly. "I'll brush 'em down and take care of their feed and water." Without waiting for a response, he left the table and hurried out the kitchen door.

"He sure looks a lot like his old man," Carlin said. "And, for a fact, he always took a liking to you—a regular little puppy dog he was, following you around." He paused. "Not with me."

"Maybe because I didn't whale on him just because he was a kid," Mitch said. "He and his pa don't forget how you acted, and neither do I."

Ed Gilchrist reappeared suddenly in the doorway, his manner hurried and alarmed. "Fellers, there's a pack of riders coming hard up the road. Reckon that's got anything to do with you folks?"

Mitch and Carlin joined the station agent at the door to look at the distant riders.

"Could be Nate Roby and the boys," Carlin said. "Matter of fact, I'd lay odds on it."

"Who are they?" Gilchrist asked.

"Bob's old gang," Mitch told him, his visage grim. "I thought we'd left them behind back in Sherman." He paused. "I guess I should've told you about them."

"Yeah, it might have been nice to have knowed," Gilchrist agreed in mild sarcasm. He looked to Carlin. "They're bad un's, are they?"

"You could rightly call 'em that," Carlin confirmed.

"My fault for getting you into this mess," Mitch said ruefully. "Sorry, I thought they'd still be hunting Bob back there in Sherman."

Gilchrist cocked his head and gave a wry smile. "Well, by golly, it does add some excitement to my day. Heaven knows, it surely gets mighty boring 'round here."

"I don't think you deserve *this* kind of excitement," Mitch told him.

Carlin raised both hands and stared at his shackled wrists. "You gonna let them get at me like this?"

"Maybe they'll move on," Mitch said, drawing his revolver. "We'll keep you out of sight in the storeroom."

"I'll go out and talk to 'em," Gilchrist volunteered. "Maybe I can steer 'em on their way."

"I don't like that, Ed," Mitch said. "This is a mean bunch, and I don't like putting you in danger."

"Been in it before," the agent countered. "I'm a pretty fair liar, and I think I can handle 'em all right."

"What if they want to come in?" Carlin questioned.

"If you keep quiet in that storeroom and they don't see me, they'll never know," Mitch told him. He caught Carlin's arm, turned him, and pushed the outlaw to the corridor at the back of the main room. "Get in there," he said as he opened a storage-room door.

"Leave the door open a bit so I can hear?" Carlin asked.

"Get in there!" Mitch repeated with an impatient wave of his revolver. Mitch shoved Carlin into the small storage room, closed the door, and locked it. He hurried to join Gilchrist at the doorway and peered past him to the road. In the near distance, five riders were slowing their horses to a slower gait as they approached the stage station. Sure enough, the outlaw Nate Roby was one of the horsemen.

"Stay close to the door," Mitch told the agent as he retreated into the room and dropped flat to the floor next to the front wall in a deeply shadowed area. "I'll cover you from back here."

"I ain't worried," Gilchrist said.

"Well, I'm worried for you just the same."

Gilchrist took two steps out of the door and raised a welcoming hand as the riders thundered toward him.

Their leader, Roby, reined up and glared down at the bald-headed man as he spoke. "Hey, old man, see a couple of riders come through here lately? Heading east?"

"Riders come through all the time," Gilchrist answered, his tone affable. "Don't know that I would've paid no attention."

Roby turned away and waved to one of the men, who nodded and spurred his horse and disappeared from view.

"Looking in the barn," Mitch said under his breath. "Hope they don't spot Pat."

"Sure you ain't seen nobody?" Roby persisted.

"Like I said, could've gone right past," Gilchrist said, easing one step, then another, toward the doorway.

"Going somewhere, baldy?"

"Figgered you might be riding on," Gilchrist said.

The absent rider reappeared in Mitch's view, riding close to Roby. "Some saddle horses in the barn, Nate. One looks like Bob's bay."

"You're a lying old coot!" Roby barked, and he snatched the revolver from his hip holster and aimed it at the station agent.

"Run, Ed!" Mitch shouted, and he snapped off a shot, the bullet ticking at the brim of Roby's hat, frightening and distracting the outlaw. Ed Gilchrist summoned an extraordinary adrenaline surge and lunged for the doorway as Roby frantically wheeled his horse away, turning in his saddle to fire repeatedly at the fleeing man. The bullets hit the doorframe and zipped through the open space as Gilchrist threw himself inside and beneath the window of the adobe-brick wall. Mitch returned fire as the outlaws whipped their horses in a wild flight away and was satisfied to see one of the men abruptly hunch forward and cry out. Moments later they were past effective handgun range, dismounting from their horses and each dashing to find cover behind trees and earth embankments.

"You okay, Ed?" Mitch asked as he crept across the floor to position himself next to the open door.

"Seem to be," Gilchrist said, rolling to his back and looking down at his body. "Knee hurts, but I think that's 'cause I banged it on the doorframe coming in." He flexed it a couple of times and smiled. "Just a tired ol' kneebone." He reached over to close the heavy plank door.

"Mitch!" came a muffled cry from the storeroom. "What's going on? Let me out!"

"Let me wriggle to the back room and get me a rifle," the agent said. "Got another one back there too." He started crawling across the floor. "Want me to let your pal out?"

"He'll keep hollering 'til we do," Mitch said. "Tell him to stay low."

Rifle shots were beginning to pepper the adobe building, and the front window was immediately shattered. A steady barrage of bullets sped into the big room, thumping into the back wall, some slamming into the kitchen and ricocheting off the big iron cookstove. Mitch cautiously opened the door a one-inch crack to peer out.

Seconds later, Gilchrist, bending low, returned to the front room with two rifles. He slid one across the floor to Mitch, a lever-action Winchester.

Mitch checked the load and poked the barrel through the narrow space between the door and the doorframe.

"You sure you want Carlin out?" Gilchrist said.

"If they get past us, it wouldn't be fair to leave him in there with no chance to get away," Mitch said, his eyes seeking a target in line with the rifle sights. "You can let him out."

There was a sound of a key turning in a lock, and then Bob Carlin appeared in a crouch in the hallway. He crept across the floor to the front of the room, keeping his head below the windowsill. He raised his head for a quick peek and ducked only a moment before a bullet thumped into the sill three inches away.

"You might want to keep your head down," Mitch said dryly.

"I'll bet that was Bud Schooley." Carlin gave an opinion. "He's probably the best rifle shot out there."

"How good are they?"

"They're handy," Carlin said. "You ought to know I wouldn't ride with anyone who couldn't shoot."

There was a pause in the shooting.

"You in the house!" a shout came from outside. "Who in tarnation are you? You a bounty hunter?"

Mitch didn't answer but turned to Gilchrist. "They think it's just me and Bob. They don't know about Pat— at least, I don't think so." He shook his head. "Hope he's all right."

"Was he carrying?" Gilchrist asked.

"Handgun," Mitch said. "He has a rifle in his scabbard. Maybe he had time to get it."

"If they don't know about him, he could circle behind and pick 'em off," Gilchrist said.

"I think he's a stranger to gunfighting," Mitch said doubtfully. "And he's too big out in the open. They'd see him easy."

"You in the house!" the voice shouted again. "You help yourself to, maybe, a thousand dollars outta that money fer your trouble, and then send out the rest with Carlin. You do that, and we'll leave you all peaceable-like."

"Your name Roby?" Mitch called out.

"If that's any of yore business!"

"This place is as thick as a fort!" Mitch shouted. "We've got food, we've got plenty of ammunition, and we've got time to pick you off any time somebody sticks his head up!"

"You ain't that good!" Roby challenged.

"Already put a shot in one of you!" Mitch countered. "I expect he's gonna need some medication or maybe even a headstone unless you get him some help!"

"He ain't all that bad hurt!"

"Be that as it may, Carlin's my prisoner, and he and the money stay inside!"

A volley of shots sounded, the bullets pounding into the adobe walls.

"Just how much ammunition *do* you have?" Carlin asked.

"What's left in my Colt and five on my belt," Mitch answered. He turned to Gilchrist. "What about your rifles?"

"A little less than a box between us," the station agent replied.

The shots from the besieging outlaws continued now in a constant onslaught. A torrent of bullets poured though the broken window, slamming into the walls with more than a few glancing and skipping dangerously around the room.

"Damn," Carlin swore, casting an accusing look at Mitch. "So you've got . . . what did you say? 'Plenty of ammunition'?"

"Wasn't exactly figuring on a war."

"Well, you've surely got one now," Carlin said.

"I think I saw one of 'em out in the back," Gilchrist warned. "There's a window open back in my bedroom. They might come in that way."

Mitch sighed in dismay. "Okay, lay flat hugging the wall and keep an eye on that hallway and the kitchen door. When they come, you'll have a field of fire either way."

"You keep Carlin and throw out the money!" Roby shouted. "That's all we want!"

"You any good with that rifle?" Carlin directed his question to Gilchrist.

"Not very," the station agent admitted.

"That means we got one gun," Carlin said to Mitch. "Yours. We've got this old gent who says he's not very good and maybe that kid hiding out Lord knows where, and I'd guess he's never shot more than a rabbit." He gestured outside with his manacled hands. "You've got five men out there who *do* know how to shoot, and that's not what I'd say are good odds." Again he raised his hands. "Take this off, and give me one of the guns."

"And that would make it six against me?" Mitch scoffed.

"You're short on bullets," Carlin said bluntly and canted his head toward Gilchrist. "You can't let the boy and the old man waste them."

Two sharp reports of Gilchrist's rifle gave significance to Carlin's caution. "Man at the back!" the agent yelled.

"You get him?" Mitch's voice was agitated. He abandoned his post at the front door and crept across the floor to peer down the hallway.

"I'm not sure," Gilchrist said uncertainly. "Maybe not."

"Give me a gun, Mitch," Carlin asked again. "Two good shooters against the bunch of them," he persisted. "You, Pat, and old Ed here got to live through this. Then you can worry about me."

"Maybe Pat isn't as poor a shot as you think," Mitch said. He crawled back to reposition himself at the wall beside the heavy front door.

"And maybe he's lying dead out in the barn," Carlin countered. "Listen, Nate Roby is a wild man. He's not right in the head, and he has no patience at all. He'd like to have me, but it's the money he's really after, and, sooner than later, he's going to rush this building and push every man with him to do the same." He cocked his head toward the station agent across the room who was peering anxiously down the hallway. "When they come, they'll come shooting, and old Ed here will be the first to die."

Gilchrist swiveled his head to glare at Carlin. "I don't die that easy."

"Won't be your fault if you do," Carlin said. "Mr. Mitch here brought you the trouble. Let me have your rifle, and I'll keep you alive."

No one spoke for several minutes, although the shots from the desperados' guns continued to pound the adobe building and whistle through the window, some dangerously near.

Finally Mitch shook his head. "Sorry, Bob. I'll take the guns I trust rather than yours that I don't."

"Your funeral," Carlin said. "And likely the same for the others."

"We'll take our chances," Gilchrist said.

"Stay under cover," Mitch told Carlin. "And out of our way."

Carlin shrugged and stretched out against a wall.

"Mitch!" A voice came from the back of the house. "It's me! Can I come in?"

"Pat? You okay?"

"Yeah, but somebody in there was shooting at me."

There was a long silence.

"Guess it's a good thing I ain't much of shot," Gilchrist said meekly.

"Anybody else back there?" Mitch called.

"Not yet," young McGrath said as he, bending low, scrambled through the back door into the hallway. "I think a couple of 'em are moving 'round."

"You get the rifle?" Mitch asked.

"Couldn't get to it, and I took a heck of a chance in getting here," Pat said. "I've got my handgun."

"How about bullets?"

"Them that's in the chambers."

"Ever kill anybody, Ed?" Carlin asked from the kitchen, flinching as a bullet thumped into the wall a half-foot above his body. He crawled closer to the cookstove.

"Nope."

"Pat?"

"No, I ain't never either."

"When it comes time to pull the trigger, you gonna do it?"

Neither the agent nor Pat answered.

"Either you or Pat hesitates, you're dead men," the outlaw told them. "Those men out there, they won't hesitate. They've killed before, and they'll shoot you while you're thinking about it."

The gunfire came to an abrupt halt, and an ominous silence prevailed.

"Hey," Ed Gilchrist said, "they've stopped shooting. Maybe they're going—"

"They're getting ready," Carlin cut in.

Mitch nodded and raised his voice. "Pat, Ed, they'll come to the house in the blind spots, and you won't see them 'til they're right on you. Pat, cover that back window. Make sure both of you are behind something solid, and keep pulling your triggers!"

Patrick gave a curt nod and crept swiftly back down the hall and turned left into the bedroom.

From the front of the house, the firing resumed, although it now appeared to be rapid reports from a single rifle.

"Covering fire!" Carlin shouted. "They'll be hugging the sides of the walls!"

Hoping for the lone shooter to reload, Mitch laid his rifle aside and gripped his Colt in his right hand. He waited 'til the rifle fire paused, then grasped the bottom of the door, swung it wider, and thrust his head and shoulders through the opening. One of the outlaws, with his back against the wall, was edging his way toward the front window. A second too late he discovered Mitch's presence and swung his revolver. Mitch, without sighting his aim, triggered a general direction shot with his revolver. Before he fired again, he saw the outlaw clutch at his chest, reel in a death throe out into the yard, and fall mortally wounded. A bullet from the distant rifleman whistled past his head as Mitch ducked back inside the building, slamming the door shut as two more shots punched into the heavy wood in front of his face.

"One down!" Mitch exulted.

At the back of the house, Pat's revolver fired three times, followed by several loud clicks of the hammer on empty chambers. "They're coming in!" Pat cried in alarm.

Simultaneously a scruffy outlaw burst through the kitchen door and hesitated, seeking a target, while at the back entrance to the hallway, a burly figure rushed into sight, lumbering forward with his revolver firing wildly left and right.

Mitch rolled from the door to a crouch and fired a shot from his Colt at the hallway intruder.

Gilchrist, flat on the floor, fired twice at the man in the kitchen and missed both times. Carlin drove his body up from behind the stove and slammed his shoulder into the surprised outlaw's midsection and knocked him against the wall as the gun flew from his hand and skittered under the stove. Gilchrist's third shot found its mark in the man's midsection, and the outlaw crumpled to the floor.

The lurching desperado in the hallway staggered and fell forward, his body landing on top of the panicked station agent. With a loud cry of dismay and abhorrence, Gilchrist shoved his way out from under the dead man, leaving his weapon behind.

Then there was silence.

"Looks like I saved your bacon, old man," Carlin said

as he rose to a crouch and looked down at the lifeless outlaw beside him.

"Is he . . . ?"

"It's okay, Ed," Mitch said to calm the frightened man. "He's dead."

"You sure?" Gilchrist's question was high-pitched and doubtful.

"There's two left," Mitch countered, turning to look out the front window. "We might yet—"

At a sudden flurry of activity behind him, he turned to see Carlin pulling Gilchrist's rifle from under the dead man in the hall, and, before he could react, Carlin brought it up, ready to fire.

"You're covered, Mitch. Lay the Peacemaker on the floor," Carlin said. "You're covered too, Ed."

"Damn you, Bob," Mitch said, still with the side arm in his hand.

"Drop it, or I'll kill Ed," Carlin said, then raised his voice. "Pat! Drop your gun and come out, or I'll kill the old man." In the back bedroom, there was a heavy thump.

"Gun on the floor, Mitch," Carlin commanded. "And slide it over to me."

Mitch lowered the Colt to the floor and slid it in an opposite direction.

Carlin gave an arched look and a shake of his head. "Hadn't made up my mind about you, Mitch, but you just did it for me." He raised his voice, "Out here, youngster, hands high!"

A moment later, Pat, with his hands raised, lumbered

slowly into the hallway entrance, lowering his hands and hunkering down as shooting began once again, a couple of bullets through the front window hammering an interior wall.

"Now, I'll take those saddlebags with my money," Carlin continued as he rose to his feet. "Fetch 'em for me, old man."

Gilchrist struggled to a crouch and cast a fearful look over the sill of the shattered window. He moved cautiously across the room to the saddlebags that were hung over the back of one of the dining area chairs.

"Your friends are still here," Mitch reminded him. "I wouldn't go out there if I were you."

"Best chance I got to cheat the hangman," Carlin said.

"They'll pick you off as soon as you show yourself," Mitch said.

"Well, there's only two left, thanks to you, and that helps my odds," Carlin said, and he turned to Gilchrist as the old man walked back with the saddlebags. "Ed, you can cozy up to me while we go out to the barn."

"You gonna use Ed for a shield?" Pat asked, his voice showing his shocked disbelief.

"Maybe take the pair of you," Carlin said with bitter mirth. "You're big enough to hide me pretty good." His eyes swept toward Mitch, and the rifle came up. "Goodbye, old friend."

Pat McGrath sprang with amazing swiftness for such a large young man, his massive right fist swinging hard against the outlaw's jaw as his left hand batted the rifle barrel down just before Carlin triggered a round into the floor. Carlin eyes were wide in shock and surprise as he crumpled, dazed.

Mitch was nearly as fast to reach the fallen man and wrest the rifle from his hands. He stayed low, mindful of the sporadic gunfire now thumping into the room. He bent down to peer into the dazed gang leader's face, making sure that the blow had taken the belligerence from him. Satisfied, he handed the rifle to Gilchrist and, in exchange, took the saddlebags from him.

"Drag him back into that storeroom, Pat," Mitch said. "I should've never let him out."

"Did I hurt him bad?" Pat asked, more curious than concerned.

"Not as bad as he deserved," Mitch barked. "We're not clear yet of those hooligans outside." After watching the woozy Carlin returned to a storeroom, he returned to a vigil next to the front door. Twice he saw a momentary glimpse of a man's head, not enough to make a viable target, but it did give him the thought that it was the same man.

"Three down," Gilchrist said, recovering his composure. "Things are getting better."

"Still two out there," Mitch responded. "Maybe."

"Maybe?"

"I winged one—how bad, I don't know," Mitch said. "That Roby said the other fellow wasn't bad hurt, but maybe he's worse off than they let on."

"So what do we do? Stay put?" Pat asked.

"I don't like the idea of being clay pigeons," Mitch countered. "One or two of them, they're still shooting, and we've already had some close calls. Sooner or later somebody's going to get hit." He rose to a crouch, opened the cylinder of his revolver, and, taking bullets from the few left on his belt, he reloaded.

"Whatcha fixing to do?" Pat asked.

"I'd rather be the hunter than the hunted."

Chapter Twenty-four

Mitch scanned the surrounding terrain from just inside the side door of the adobe building. There was a great temptation to remain inside, to not take the risk of exposure. However, continuing sniper gunfire posed a greater jeopardy: sooner or later a direct hit or a ricochet would find one of them, resulting in a kill or a bad injury.

"Keep your eyes on the front and back," he said to Ed and Pat. "I think we've got the edge now, but don't count on it. So far I haven't seen Roby, so I assume he's still active."

"You think there's two of 'em left?"

"I'm hoping that there's just Roby and another out of action," Mitch said.

214

"Uh, Mitch," Pat began uncertainly, "what if you don't come back?"

Mitch took a long look at the wooded area behind the station facility and nodded. "Then I'd say the two of you ought to leave the money and hightail it into those woods. Run far, and hide good."

"What about Bob?"

He handed the manacle key to Pat. "Leave this, and tell him where he can find it, then unlock the storeroom as you go out the back door."

"Should I leave him a gun?"

Mitch shrugged. "I don't think I would, but that'll be up to the two of you." He turned away and resumed his surveillance of the stable enclosure. He pointed to the edge of the work yard where, thirty yards distant, a growth of locust and pine trees rose atop a terrain of small knolls and mounds. "You've got a couple of extra guns now. Start firing a few shots to get their attention. When I hear them, I'll make a run for those trees."

Nodding their assent, Pat and Ed scrabbled their way toward the front of the building, and seconds later both began firing their weapons.

With a final look left and right, with his revolver in hand, Mitch went through the side door and, running low, dashed halfway across the open space to crouch behind a low water trough. He remained there for a few seconds, then resumed his sprint for the shelter of the trees.

The sound of gunshots continued, although Mitch had no sense that any bullet had sped near him. Nonetheless, he felt great relief as he threw himself behind a protective earthen mound next to the thick trunk of a substantial locust tree. He rose and moved stealthily toward the road, his eyes searching for swells and hollows of the ground to shield him from fire as he sought to circle behind the assailants.

As he advanced, he noticed that the gunfire was now quite infrequent, only the report of a rifle or handgun from time to time and now only from inside the adobe building. He moved from cover to cover, coming wide around the station complex where, at last, he discovered several of the outlaws' horses wandering and grazing in a grassy area, reins dragging. Looking in the general direction where he'd last glimpsed Nate Roby, he saw no sign of him. He looked again at the horses and counted four, the fifth missing.

Mitch lowered his revolver, although he remained cautious and alert. He waited patiently, watching for human movement and noting the cessation of gunshots from the building. As chaotic and perilous as the scene had been only minutes before, there was now only the quite serenity of a summer day.

After ten minutes he holstered his sidearm, cupped his hands to his mouth, and called, "In the house! Hold your fire! I think it's over!"

Guardedly he ventured into the area where the outlaws

had mounted their initial assault and found a body curled in a final, fetal pose. He bent close to make sure of the outlaw's death and then, still wary, crossed quickly to the front door of the building.

"I think Roby's gone," Mitch said as he stepped inside. "I don't know if and when he left or why."

"Maybe I do," Gilchrist said. "Let me show you something." He walked outside and gestured for Mitch to follow.

Puzzled and still vigilant, Mitch stepped to the doorway and no farther. "Ed, I wouldn't—"

"Look there," the agent cut in, and he raised a hand high above his head.

Mitch started to repeat his warning, but the words never left his mouth as he gazed out at the immediate landscape. Somewhere near twenty young men stood in an arc surrounding the station, clad in store-bought work clothes, their golden-brown faces framed in wide-brimmed western and straw hats.

"Where did they—?"

"Some of my Chickasaws," Gilchrist said, interrupting. "Heard the shooting and came to see what was going on." He raised his hand again and waved. "Maybe to see if I was all right."

"They friendly?" Pat asked, moving up to stand behind Mitch.

"Have been to me," Gilchrist said.

"You think they ran Roby off?" Mitch asked.

The station agent nodded and grinned. "'Spect he thought they was gonna scalp him."

"I hope they did," Pat put in. "Think they let him go?"

"I 'spect so." Gilchrist laughed. "They just came to see the fight, but that hooligan thought they might take sides ag'in him."

As they watched, the Indians began to walk away, and a few seconds later all had disappeared. The two men entered the front door and looked over the damaged interior. Bullet holes pocked the walls, broken glass covered the floor beneath the window frame, the whiskey bottles on the small shelf had been shattered, and the brown liquid was dripping down into an expanding pool. The chairs in the fireplace area were battered and broken, a small table overturned, and a coal-oil lamp lay in pieces nearby. The kitchen cupboards were riddled with holes and, inside, tin plates and cups were dented or shot through. A few bullets had hit the cane chairs, but neither they nor the heavy plank table were badly damaged.

"It's quite a mess, Ed," Mitch observed. "We'll take some of the cash from the saddlebags to pay for it."

"Mainly to replace the glass," Gilchrist said. "I'll have the fellers on the next stage get me some new panes, and me and Joseph can patch 'er together."

"Well, we've got to clean up," Pat said. "I'll get Bob out of storage to lend a . . . both hands."

"One thing more," Ed Gilchrist interposed. "You

fellers chance to pass through here some time in the future . . ."

Mitch and Pat turned attentively to the older man, who was now wearing a rueful grin.

". . . appreciate it if you keep right on riding."

Chapter Twenty-five

Days later, as the sphere of the next morning's sun cleared the horizon, Pat McGrath finished tying his bedroll behind the saddle on his horse, then turned to offer a huge hand to Mitch. "You sure you ain't gonna need me to ride along?"

Mitch clasped the young man's hand and squeezed it tightly. "I owe you, your pa, and your mom," he said. "You've got a long trip, so you head on home. Your family's likely been worrying, and you need to show yourself, fit and hardy."

"I still think—"

"It's only a half day's ride from here to Harrisonville at the most," Mitch interrupted him. "Besides, there's going to be a lot of questions asked, and if there's any doubt about me, I don't want you to get caught up in it."

220

"Well, you've got Bob and the money and that woman and—"

"And Bob will lie and tell them you and me were members of his gang," Mitch cut in again. "I've got a prison record, and, Lordy, that woman there at Mayfield may or may not speak up for me. It's better that you get clear of this."

"You'll let us know?"

"If they believe me, I'll pay another visit," Mitch assured him. "If you don't hear, you'll know I'm back in the Jeff City pen."

"Prayers go with you," Pat said, and he took his hand away. He moved to his horse and swung his big body up into the saddle. "Think they'll ever catch that Roby feller?"

Mitch shrugged. "We can hope." He stepped closer to Pat's horse and pointed at the coiled lariat hanging from the saddle. "Mind if I borrow that?"

Pat untied the rawhide rope and handed the coil down to Mitch. "Whatcha going to do with it?" he asked.

"Plan to keep Mr. Carlin on a harness," Mitch answered. "Take care as you go, young fellow. You've got a long way to get home."

Pat raised a hand in a farewell salute and rode his horse away.

Mitch watched until the horse and rider disappeared from sight. He turned to his captive, who sat quietly and dejectedly on his horse, his eyes cast down. Surprised at his own feelings, Mitch experienced a sense of regret, almost sorrow for the man who had once been his valued childhood companion. Bob's defiance and bravado had ebbed over the past few days, and now, thirty miles from home territory, he seemed to have given up. Earlier in the journey, as they traveled, Mitch had watched the outlaw's eyes darting this way and that, his grave expression revealing the mind behind those eyes seeking some way to escape. Now that spirit seemed to have fled, leaving, perhaps, pathos.

"Buck up, Bob," Mitch said in a low voice. "Maybe it won't go so bad for you."

Carlin's head came up, and, in a flashing temper, the defiance reappeared. "As if you give a damn?"

"Whether I do or don't, let's get a move on."

"And if I don't?"

"Sitting in the saddle or lying across it—your choice."

They glared at each other for several seconds.

With an exaggerated sigh, Carlin booted his horse to a walk toward the road, his right hand cuffed to the saddle horn. Mitch mounted Belle and guided his mare to follow a few feet behind. They rode in silence for several miles, Carlin seemingly docile, his gaze idly roving over the lush greenery of the surrounding countryside.

Mitch, however, was keenly aware that these last miles into Harrisonville posed the final and greatest temptation

for Carlin to try an escape. He had pondered what action he would take if his outlaw companion spurred his
horse into a gallop and made a run for it. He could shoot
the man and lose a valued asset for proving his own innocence. He could shoot the horse, an act of cruelty to
the animal and a time-delay inconvenience. There was
one alternative.

He unfastened the lariat from his saddle, slipped open
a loop, and rode up behind the unsuspecting Carlin.
With an expert swing of the lasso, he cast it over Carlin's
head and torso and then pulled it tight, nearly hauling the
man from his horse. Mitch looped the line loosely around
the horn of his own saddle to allow slippage or a fast hold
if necessary, the remaining coil of the lariat held in his
gloved left hand.

"What the hell!" Carlin shouted, struggling against
the lasso.

"Leave it be!" Mitch said in a loud voice. "You try a
run, and I'll yank you clean out of your saddle!"

"I'm riding thirty miles like this?"

"I know you, Bob," Mitch said. "Wear it easy or, I
swear, I'll hogtie you hand and foot if I have to."

"You're going to make me ride into town like a cur on
a leash?"

"Whatever's necessary."

They rode on, hour upon hour, Carlin, at times when
the lasso seemed slack, trying to wriggle the noose higher
on his body.

"Keep trying that," Mitch called, pulling the rope tighter, "and you'll hang yourself."

"Might as well be here as where we're going."

At the near side of the wooden bridge, they rode their horses down a gentle slope of the embankment and stopped in the welcome shade of the trees overhanging the river. Mitch swung down from his saddle and allowed Carlin to shrug off the lariat and dismount from his bay. They watched for a few minutes while the horses drank at the water's edge, both men wiping sweat away with their neckerchiefs.

"Missouri summers, hot as Hades," Carlin said, and he inclined his head toward a path running alongside the flowing river. "You mind if we go upstream a bit and find a place to cool off?"

"Long as you don't try anything foolish," Mitch said.

Mitch tied the reins of both horses to a tree several feet away from the water and then, walking several paces behind Carlin, followed him on the bare earth trail. The pathway wound along the course of the river, and around a bend sixty yards upstream from the bridge they came to a hollow in the bank where the water eddied in a pool, a lazy swirl flowing clear and cool over a stony bed a half foot below.

As his prisoner knelt by the pool to splash the day's heat from his neck and face, Mitch glanced through the leafy crown above to find the position of the sun. No more than twelve miles now from Harrisonville; he estimated they would reach their destination no later than four o'clock that afternoon. There had been no dialogue between them other than Mitch's curt commands and Carlin's swear-word responses. For the most part Mitch felt that the fight had gone out of his captive and a resignation had come in its stead.

Nonetheless, when he took his turn at the pool, he kept a watchful eye on Carlin and his right hand near his holstered gun as, with his left, he dipped his bandanna into the cool water. He sponged the dust from his face, dipped the kerchief once again, removed his hat, and draped it over his head. A minute later he rose and, with a curt slant of his head, motioned Carlin to precede him back along the path to his horse.

They were walking single file along the path when Nate Roby came out of a thicket, his appearance so swift and unexpected that it took crucial seconds for Mitch to shift his eyes from Carlin and the trail to the intruder and the danger. Roby's revolver was already aimed at him, and death was a trigger-pull away.

Carlin, inadvertently or purposely, stepped into the line of fire and took the bullet, his body a shield lasting long enough for Mitch to whip the Colt from his holster. As Carlin sagged to the ground, Mitch fired three times, two bullets striking the dumbfounded cutthroat, whose eyes rolled up in his head as he toppled facedown and did not stir.

With an anguished glance at Carlin, Mitch moved quickly past him to the fallen assailant and, with his revolver raised and ready, leaned down to feel for a pulse at the man's neck. He hovered over the hooligan to ascertain death, nodded a confirmation, holstered his side arm, and then hastened back to kneel beside Carlin.

"Bob, what the hell did you do?" he asked. He looked down at the spreading blood seeping through Carlin's shirt.

Carlin's eyes fluttered, and a red-tinged froth bubbled from his mouth as he labored to speak, his voice only a whisper. "Lift me up . . . can't breathe."

Mitch slid his left arm under the fallen man's shoulders and raised his head and upper chest from the ground. "What did you do?" he repeated.

A half smile came to Carlin's lips. "Must've . . . stepped . . . wrong way."

"Hang on, Bob," Mitch said, looking up the path to the horses. "It's not far into town—"

"Too far," whispered the faint voice. "A million miles—" His words choked off as a gush of blood flooded into his mouth and trickled down each side of his chin, and Carlin's eyes closed.

For a moment Mitch thought he was gone.

Then the eyes came open again, although Carlin's voice was barely there, hard to hear. "When I shot you . . . did it hurt?"

Mitch didn't immediately respond and then nodded.

"Funny, I don't . . . hurt . . . much at all."

"You really didn't . . . step wrong," Mitch said.

"Killed us both . . . anyway," Carlin whispered haltingly. "Better . . . than . . . noose." A crimson smile came to his lips. "And . . . I still owe—"

There was a sudden stiffening of Carlin's body, his eyes bulging, and a shuddering. Then a gasp came and held for a long few moments, followed by a lingering exhalation as he slumped down into Mitch's arm. Carlin's lips moved, and Mitch leaned close, his ear an inch away to hear words on a final sighing breath.

Then Mitch slowly leaned back and repeated in a whisper of his own, "Frying pan." He nodded, and, to his surprise, his eyes misted. He sat for a long while, his left arm still cradling the body, staring at the ripples, swirls, and cascades of the nearby river. Finally he laid Carlin gently on the path. He rose and looked down at the two dead men for several minutes, then turned back along the path to where the horses were contentedly grazing. His eyes fastened on the saddlebags that contained the bank money still on Carlin's bay, and briefly he considered how differently it might have been if only Roby had taken it and gone. Instead, murder had prevailed.

He walked back up the embankment and searched the area until he found Roby's horse tethered some distance back along the road in a grove of trees. He led the horse to tie it with the other two mounts, reached into his jeans for a pocket knife, and used it to cut his lariat into several lengths. Then he trudged down the slope to retrieve the bodies.

Chapter Twenty-six

Pedestrians on the main street of Harrisonville stopped and gaped at the sight of a bearded man on horseback leading two other steeds with bodies lying crosswise over the saddles and securely lashed to the animals. By the time the rider and his trailing burdens reached the city jail, quite a number of the townspeople had followed them, and two men with badges were already on the boardwalk to see what it was all about.

"Looking for the sheriff," Mitch said, still astride his horse.

"I'm Sheriff Todd," the large, ruddy-face man said. "Who you got here?"

"Bob Carlin and Nathan Roby—a couple of the fellows who robbed your bank," Mitch said, and he pointed to the saddlebags behind Carlin's saddle. "You'll find most of the bank's money in there."

"And what's your part in this?" the sheriff questioned, his manner becoming stern and officious.

"I'm Mitchell Ellsworth from over in Laclede County outside of Lebanon," Mitch said. "I may be a wanted man."

"Mitchell Ellsworth." The sheriff repeated the name, musing over it. He drew his revolver and then nodded to his deputy. "Bert, take those bodies over to the funeral parlor, and tell Bill I'll be over later." He moved closer to Mitch's horse and reached up to him. "I'll take your handgun while we sort all this out."

Mitch nodded and carefully removed the Colt from his holster and handed it to the lawman. He dismounted and tied Belle to a hitching rail, turning his head to watch as the deputy, Bert, led the horses with the bodies away.

"Step into the jail, and we'll talk about what you've been doing," the sheriff said.

They entered the jail office, a small room with a desk at one side, a rifle rack and wooden file cabinets at the other. In between, an open door revealed four cells on either side of a central aisle. Sheriff Todd motioned Mitch into a chair across from the desk at the right side of the room. He seated himself behind the desk, his manner genial, yet he continued to hold the revolver in his right hand.

"Marshal Langley over there in Mayfield has a warrant out for your arrest," the sheriff told him.

Mitch wondered about the sham grave at the old Ellsworth burial site, but he remained silent.

The sheriff gave a slight, knowing smile. "That Jennings lady who gave you care and old Doc Davis . . . they came over here a few days after you left and told me what they did to help you."

"Are they in trouble?"

The sheriff shrugged. "Can't say that they're not. Marshal Langley is making a fuss about it. He was mad as hell 'cause they came to tell me, but more because they fooled him. He wants to jail both of 'em and set 'em up for trial." He paused. "That didn't set well with the townfolk over there, since Doc Davis is the only medicine man for their sick'uns. They also didn't like the idee of a widow lady being put into that smelly old jail over there."

"Did they tell what really happened?"

"The Jennings told her story and said you couldn't have been with the gang when they robbed the bank 'cause she found you shot before the whole danged thing went down."

"Where does that leave me?"

The sheriff pursed his lips, a look of regret on his face. "Trouble is, with just that lady's say-so, it's only her word that seems to clear you." He paused. "Some even say it was because she's lonely and she was sweet on you."

Mitch gave a sigh of disgust. "Lordy, that's just plain

nonsense! Mrs. Jennings, she didn't know me from Adam, and she sure didn't find anything 'sweet' about me. In fact, she was downright suspicious of me."

"Then why did she let you go?"

"Because she knew I wasn't with the Carlin gang, and she also knew that that so-called lawman, Marshal Langley, would've let me die, not given me a fair trial."

"I'm still going to have to put you in lockup 'til we know the straight of everything."

"What about my bringing back the money and two of the men who really robbed your bank?" Mitch asked, a slight edge of irritation in his voice.

"That's to your favor, I admit," the sheriff agreed. "Still, you *do* have a record."

Mitch gave another sigh of exasperation. "So what happens now?"

"We got a judge here in town—fair man of good character," Todd said. "We'll have the arraignment and set up a prelim hearing and see what everybody's got to say."

Mitch cast his eyes down at the floor and shook his head. "Chances are, nothing good will come of that."

Chapter Twenty-seven

"Court's in session! Honorable Judge Clayton Swann presiding! Everybody rise!" The acting bailiff made his announcements in a voice louder than necessary for the assembly of men and one woman seated in the front few pews of the Methodist church. The people stood while a hefty, bald-headed, middle-aged man wearing a dark suit, white shirt, and narrow tie walked from the left aisle of the church nave to seat himself in a straight-backed chair behind a wooden table placed in the front of the narthex. He picked up a gavel from the table and rapped it sharply three times.

"That's okay, Bert," the judge said to the sheriff's deputy. "Let's not make a big show out of this." He waved both hands. "You all sit." He waited as the people sat again in the front rows of pews. "Technically you'd call this a preliminary hearing, but we're just going to listen to some folks and see if we can't make heads or tails out of what's been going on. We'll be just kinda informal in these proceedings."

It was a small church with a raised pulpit at the left side of the narthex, nine empty chairs at the right for a choir, and an upright piano against the right wall. There were seven high-backed pews on either side of a central aisle and a side aisle along each wall of the narrow building's interior.

Seated on the right front bench, Mitch Ellsworth had a nervous young man by his side. In the second pew, Susan Jennings sat with Dr. Leonard Davis and three other men, citizens of Harrisonville, who had come to testify.

In the left front pew, Sheriff Willard Todd sat with a wide space separating him from a tall, pudgy man in soiled work clothes with a badge on his shirt—Mayfield's town marshal, Orville Langley. Behind them sat another two Harrisonville witnesses. At the back of the church, the pastor sat in a chair in the entry vestibule.

"Due to the repairs going on at the courthouse, we're mighty grateful to have the use of Reverend Bradley's fine church for this hearing," Judge Swann told them. He looked around, his manner indicating an appreciation of the small house of worship. He finished his survey and then looked at the young man sitting next to Mitch. "You here officially, Charlie?"

Sheriff Todd came to his feet and nodded. "Since we

only got one other law fellow here in town, other than you, Clay, I thought I'd give him to Mr. Ellsworth here if he needs him."

"Maybe so, maybe not," the judge said.

The slim young man, no more than twenty-five, rose uncertainly. "Charles W. Hoffman . . . I am representing the defendant, Mr. Wallace Mitchell Ellsworth." He smiled and turned to Mitch, sitting beside him. "We want to plead—"

"Just a minute, Charlie," the judge interrupted. "You want to go first, Will?"

"If you say so, sir."

"Then proceed, if you will."

"So many things have happened, Clay, I'm not just sure where I should start," the sheriff said. He pointed to Mitch. "Should I start with him bringing the dead bank robbers to town?"

"Good place to start would be at the beginning," Judge Swann advised. "I'd go back there."

Sheriff Todd pondered the suggestion for a few seconds and then nodded. "Well, then, I'd like to call Mrs. William Jennings to tell what she—"

"Hey, what about me?" Marshal Langley stood up. "I'm the one doing the complaining 'bout that jailbird outlaw! Don't I get the first say-so?"

Mitch leaned forward to look across the aisle, but his youthful attorney laid a placating hand on his shoulder, and he leaned back.

"Sit yourself down, Langley," the judge said sharply.

"I'll give you your say when I see fit." He nodded to Sheriff Todd. "Bring on Mrs. Jennings."

Susan Jennings, wearing a plain and simple gray muslin dress, rose to her feet and, uncertainly, glanced around.

"You can give testimony standing right there, ma'am," the judge told her. "Go ahead."

"My first encounter with Mr. Ellsworth," she began with a glance at Mitch, "was on the morning of the eighth of June, this summer." She paused and spoke again. "He rode into the yard, and he was very badly hurt. My boy— that's Andy—and I, we knew he needed a doctor right away, so we loaded him into a wagon and drove him into town to Dr. Davis."

"And how had he been hurt, ma'am?" the judge asked.

"It was a gunshot wound, was what he said, and that's what the doctor also told me," she answered.

"Shot while he was robbing the bank!" Langley interjected. "That woman ain't to be trusted."

"You interrupt again, Marshal, and you'll be the one facing charges," the judge admonished. "Continue, ma'am."

The Jennings woman gave a brief account of her trip to Mayfield and the initial medical care given by the doctor.

"May I say something, your honor?" Dr. Davis said, raising his hand.

"If you think now's the time," Judge Swann said with an approving nod.

"Young Mitchell was in dire shape," the physician said as he pushed himself up to his feet. "It was obvious that the wound had been bleeding for some time. He was danged near white as a sheet and—"

"Excuse me, Doc," the judge gently interrupted. "May I ask why this is important?"

"I'd like to answer that," Susan Jennings said quickly. "Mr. Ellsworth showed up in my yard at five minutes after ten in the morning."

"Is this proper, Clay?" Sheriff Todd asked. "Having both witnesses talking at the same time?"

"Let me worry about that, Will," the magistrate said. "Go on, ma'am."

"Well, from what's been reported, the bank robbery took place here in Harrisonville at ten-fifteen that morning," she resumed. "And I went to Marshal Langley and told him that it was impossible for Mr. Ellsworth to have been at my place and at the bank at approximately the same time."

"And what did he say?" Swann asked.

"He wouldn't listen," she said. "I got mad, but I didn't know what else to do."

"How'd you know the time?" the judge asked.

"I saw it on the mantel clock just a minute or two before I heard Mr. Ellsworth ride into the yard."

"That jibes with my estimate of when he was shot," the doctor interjected. "I figure he was shot at least an hour, maybe two, before the robbers even showed up at the bank."

"Now, wait just a damned minute!" Marshal Langley stood up and threw an angry hand gesture at the judge. "How'd that woman know her dadburned clock wasn't off by an hour or even more?"

"No swearing in my court, and, besides, you're in a church, and that makes it twice as bad or even worse," Judge Swann admonished. "I'm thinking of holding you in contempt."

"I don't care," the big man blustered. "I'll swear in court or in church—anywhere's I want."

"Sit down, and shut up!" the judge ordered. "Will, take him down to the jail if he hollers once more."

The big man started to say something, but a stern look from Sheriff Todd froze him. With more under-the-breath muttering, he resumed his seat in the second row.

"Now, Mrs. Jennings," the judge said, turning to the woman, "you, yourself, have some things to explain." He indicated Mitch with a nod of his head. "You nursed this man and then aided him to escape. Now, that not only makes your testimony somewhat suspect, but it just might call for a charge against you."

"I can explain that, your honor," she said promptly. "I was content to leave Mr. Ellsworth in the care of Dr. Davis—until I learned what Marshal Langley did to him."

"I've heard this story, but you tell it to us, and I'll see if it sounds the same," Judge Swann said.

"My boy and I were in town shopping in the general store, and I heard about what was happening out in the street," she said. "They said they were taking pictures of the bank robbers who'd been killed. I came out to see, and there was Mr. Ellsworth, propped up in a coffin, and we all thought he had passed away—"

"Marshal Langley and some men had come running up my steps," Dr. Davis cut in. "They pulled my patient off the examining table and took him downstairs. I objected strenuously, but that ignorant lout wouldn't listen. What he did was dreadful—a cruel and inhuman thing to do."

"What's a 'lout'?" Langley whispered to one of the men in the pew behind him.

"When I heard he was still alive, I went to Dr. Davis and told him it was a horrible thing they were doing," Susan Jennings said, "and that we had to do something, or the poor man would die right out there in the street."

"So you snuck him out of town and took him to your place—is that it?" the judge summed up. "I can see that, all right, but what about letting him go afterward?"

"Well, I knew if the marshal got hold of him again, they'd give him no care, and he wouldn't live to have a fair trial," she explained.

"I freely admit I had a hand in it, your honor," Dr. Davis volunteered. "If you're going to blame Susan, then you'd better charge me the same. I was the one who told her to take care of him, and, by golly, I also told her that if he got well, she should let him go on his way."

"I'd like to say that the doctor was also the one who said we had to come to Sheriff Todd here and tell him the truth," Susan Jennings added. "All we wanted was to save this man's life . . . and see that justice was done."

The judge didn't speak for a long while, and there was a resultant silence among the people in the church. Finally he nodded. "You two can sit down now." He turned to the young attorney. "You got anything for the defense?"

"Looks like the prosecution's doing just fine," Charles W. Hoffman said with a sly grin on his face. "However, I'd like to have Mr. Benjamin Williamson, the president of the Harrisonville bank, and Mr. Harry Fowler testify as to the events of June eighth of this year."

"Well, we'll bring these witnesses on one at a time," the magistrate declared. "Everybody speaking at the same time is hurting my ears and trying my patience."

One by one, the bank president, a bank teller, and five men who had witnessed the robbery testified that Mitchell Ellsworth had not been a participant in the bank holdup. After a short break for lunch the participants gathered again in the church nave.

"Well," Judge Swann began as he seated himself, "what else have we got?"

"I can let Mr. Ellsworth tell his story," Charles W. Hoffman said.

"I read his deposition," the judge said. "You got anything you want to add, Mr. Ellsworth?"

Mitch shook his head.

"Then I think we've got all we need," Swann said. "Ed, there doesn't seem to be enough here to go to a full trial."

"Wait just a . . . goldarned minute!" Marshal Langley exploded. "Don't I get to say my say?"

"Don't see a need," the judge said curtly. "From what I know about you and the way you run your job there in Mayfield, I do not consider you a credible witness." He stopped speaking for a few moments but did not break his intense stare at the beefy lawman. "Furthermore, I strongly suggest that you immediately resign your office. Should you not do so by the end of this week, I will ask for your indictment."

"On what charges?" Langley challenged.

"Drunkenness, dereliction of duty, degradation and endangerment of prisoners," Swann said. "If those don't do it, we'll find other, infractions, I'm sure." He turned his attention back to the assemblage. "Will, Charlie, ladies and gentlemen, thank you for your attendance here today. I'm dismissing all charges against Mr. Ellsworth on the basis of a lack of evidence tying him to any participation in the June eighth robbery of the Harrisonville National Bank."

Everyone rose, and there was an immediate hubbub of good cheer, shaking of hands, and exchanges of congratulations. The only dissident, Marshal Langley, roughly elbowed his way out of the pew to the center aisle and, with words seldom if ever uttered in a sanctuary, stalked to the door and out into the street.

The gavel came down three more times.

The congratulatory din sharply turned to silence as the group turned to the judge.

"One more thing," Judge Swann said. He pointed a finger at the bank president. "Ben, isn't there something you want to offer Mr. Ellsworth?"

The bank president's wide smile faded. "Why, uh, I'm not sure. . . ."

"Come on now, Ben," the judge admonished. "Seems to me there was a reward offered for information leading to the arrest of the perpetrators of this robbery."

The bank president didn't answer immediately, then cleared his throat. "Well, yes. In the amount of five thousand dollars."

"To which Mr. Ellsworth is eminently entitled," the judge declared, and he banged down his gavel. "Case dismissed."

"All rise!" sang out the deputy.

All standing looked mystified.

"Ah, Bert, for Chris—" Judge Swann said, choking off a word with a glance at the church ceiling.

Chapter Twenty-eight

It was the place where they had played as small boys: an unexpected, odd plot of ground with a cluster of knobby hillocks eroded into curious, dramatic contours by a small wandering stream. It was almost hidden by an enclosing swirl of cottonwood and poplar trees, a secret space for imaginative lads to make mounds and hummocks into battle summits against marauding Indians, ridges and knolls into fortifications against the flaming breaths of scaly dragons.

Mitch tied Belle to a tree and then walked to the far end of the enclosure, the cottonwoods and poplars now showing early flecks of red and gold leaves amid the remaining green foliage of the fading summer. He stood for a long time looking down at the mound of freshly turned earth with the granite headstone that marked the grave nestled at the apex of the clearing, unobtrusively placed to avoid marring the serenity and beauty of the woodland. He heard the approach of light footsteps and knew that it was Susan Jennings coming up behind him.

He turned and welcomed her with a nod and a smile. "The stonemason did a good job," he said. "The name and the dates and the inscription . . . all just right."

"I saw you turn in from up at the house," she said in her soft, caring voice. "Perhaps I shouldn't have come down. I wonder if you might've wanted to be alone."

Mitch shook his head. "Actually, I'm glad you came. I planned to stop by your house before I left, but your being here, at Bob's grave—I think it's the right place to thank you for all you've done for me . . . and for this."

"To be honest, I don't know why you wanted it," she responded. "With what he did . . ." She shrugged.

"I don't know that I can explain it myself," he agreed. "Maybe because . . . things once were right . . . right here."

"They wouldn't allow the burial in the town cemetery," Susan said, her voice tinged with regret. "Said it wasn't fitting for . . . for what he was."

"I think he'd like it here," Mitch said. "We couldn't bury him where he used to call home, but this is as close as we . . . as *you* could let him rest." He gestured with his left hand. "The Carlin property was just on the other side of this grove and the house up on the hill."

"New folks live there. They built a new house," she said. "They wouldn't have—"

"No, I know, and we couldn't have asked," he gently interrupted. "It was good of you to allow him here. As I've said before, you're a kind lady."

They turned and walked away from the grave, crossing back to the break in the trees. Mitch untied Belle and led her behind him as they left the grove and started across the pasture, following the well-worn footpath he had traveled so many years before.

"What will you do now?" Susan asked.

"I'll go back home to let my folks know that I'm all right," he told her. "For most of the summer they thought I was dead and buried." He gave a rueful smile. "Then I need to make another trip down to Arkansas before winter sets in. I owe some folks for what they did to help me when I needed it."

They talked of the events of the hearing and of the jubilation of Mayfield's citizens at the news of Marshal Langley's resignation. When they reached the yard of the house, Mitch turned silent, his gaze roving over the buildings, the familiarity of his childhood home seeping into his psyche.

Noting Susan's quiet, knowing observance, he walked her to the back door, where he stopped. "I'd best be on my way," he told her. "I've wired my folks, and they're eager to see me."

"What will you do with the rest of your life, Mitch Ellsworth?" Her question was a bit of a challenge.

"Try to make it as simple and ordinary as I possibly

can," he replied. "Become nothing but a plain old uncomplicated bore."

"Will you ever come back this way?"

He looked at her, not sure how to answer. "It's . . . well, it's home country to me, and that's the good part, but there's lots of hurtful memories that cling to it." He hesitated. "I know you've heard a lot of bad things about me, and most are true." He paused. "But just maybe you've come to know some other, better things about me."

She did not respond immediately, and then said, "I think you've paid for the bad things, and, just maybe"—she smiled—"you're not as bad as you and others might think."

He stood regarding her for some time, and a wry smile came to his lips. "If I should come this way again . . . would you consider it improper for me to call upon you?"

She didn't answer immediately, a slight flush rising to her cheeks. Then, with a confident tilt of her head, she smiled. "I wouldn't consider that improper at all," she said, her voice strong and frank. "I would like that . . . Mitchell. I would consider your visit . . . and your calling on me . . . a very welcome pleasure."

With an awkward sort of an acknowledging bow, Mitch turned and stepped into the stirrup of his saddle and swung up onto his horse. "It would please me as well . . . Susan."

With a nod of good-bye, he tugged the reins to turn his mount toward the road and urged Belle into a canter.

As he rode through the gate, he looked back to see that Susan was still standing in the same place, and as she saw his look, she raised a hand to wave.

"Handsome woman," he said, leaning forward to confide his thoughts to Belle as they traveled down this memorable country road. "Handsome? Hell, she's pretty!"